Date Due WEBSTER

2 5 MAY 2006

2 1 APR 2010

eILL:NNRL
9 DEC 13

OPERATION TORCH

OPERATION TORCH

Duncan Harding

severn
House

This first world edition published in Great Britain 2005 by
SEVERN HOUSE PUBLISHERS LTD of
9–15 High Street, Sutton, Surrey SM1 1DF.
This first world edition published in the USA 2005 by
SEVERN HOUSE PUBLISHERS INC of
595 Madison Avenue, New York, N.Y. 10022.

British Library Cataloguing in Publication Data

Harding, Duncan, 1926-
  Operation torch
  1. Operation Torch - Fiction
  2. World War, 1939-1945 - Campaigns - Africa, North - Fiction
  3. War stories
  I. Title
  823.9'14 [F]

  ISBN-10 : 0-7278-6263-4

Typeset by Palimpsest Book Production Ltd.,
Polmont, Stirlingshire, Scotland.
Printed and bound in Great Britain by
MPG Books Ltd., Bodmin, Cornwall.

'The whole history of the world is summed up in the fact that, when nations are strong, they are not always just, and when they wish to be just, they are no longer strong.'

Winston Churchill

'We failed to see that the leader in a democracy has to keep the people entertained.'

General Marshall,
US Chief-of-Staff, to his generals, 1942

Author's Note

Right from the start it was a cock-up. A real All-American cock-up. I don't think anybody can deny that, gentle reader.

I mean, look at the situation back then in the summer of '42. Seven long months after the Nips had attacked the Yanks, with the three Axis powers, Japan, Germany and Italy, at war with the USA, what does the Yank President Roosevelt decide to do? I'll tell you. He decides to invade French North Africa of all bloody places: neutral country, not at war with the USA, and America's major ally in World War One. Hell, years after that war, the American vets who fought were still singing that old ear-worm about '*Have a care . . . for the Yanks are coming, over . . . over there!*'

Out of the blue in July '42, the President summoned his chief-of-staff General Marshall and told him he had a whole week to prepare for an invasion of French North Africa. One hundred and fifty thousand soldiers would be carried in three hundred or so ships over 5,000 miles. Marshall, the supposed hard-arsed realist, trotted off dutifully to carry out his master's crazy order. Mind you, dear reader, the Southern General couldn't have been too much of a realist. Weeks later when he personally flew to North Africa, he arrived draped in mosquito netting to ward off the non-existent North African mosquito. And just to make sure he was prepared and had gotten the right type of climate, his plane contained a full set of Arctic gear, including snow shoes. That must have been a bit of an eye-opener for the British generals, clad in shirt-sleeves and baggy shorts, waiting to greet him. But, I suppose, by then they must have become used to the funny ways of the Yanks, who didn't even seem to speak the same language as they did.

The assault, with the British Army contingent dressing up in American uniforms to please the Yanks and appease their former allies, the anti-British French, was to be called 'Operation Torch'. Naturally the name came from Shakespeare – no other English writer would do for America's first venture into the murky world of the Middle East. The planners thought the name would inspire the 'natives', ie the frogs, not only in North Africa, but also on the French mainland, to rise and fight for their freedom. After all, the flaming torch signified liberty. It would inspire the French and signify that the Americans, their long-time friends, were coming to free them from the Nazi Yoke.

None of the planners, however, had seemed to consider that these French North Africans, who had tamely surrendered to the Nazis back in June '40, might not want to be liberated. After all, they were on a cushy number in North Africa, far from war-torn Europe. There was cheap living, plenty of cheaper sex (especially if you didn't object to black and brown women), plenty of opportunities to make money, even if it was 'tainted' Nazi marks, oodles of Arab servants who waited on them hand and foot for a pittance. Indeed, most of these *'colons'* wanted to leave things as they were, thank you very much. Why should they welcome these big-footed, uncouth Anglo-Saxons barging into their country bringing with them war and mayhem, destroying precious vineyards and orange groves?

Indeed, the only people in French North Africa who sought 'liberation' that autumn of '42 were the 'beni-yes-yeses', as the *colons* called the Arabs contemptuously. But 'A-rabs', as the Yanks named the native people, didn't fit into the equation, that is if the Americans knew that such folk even existed. The 'Torch', that sacred flame, didn't apply to them.

Chanting those words of basic French that the troops were learning by rote, *'Nous sommes soldats, Americains. Nous sommes vos amis,'* they would be welcomed as liberators by cheering crowds of white people. For the last year or so they had seen it all before in the movies that Hollywood had been feeding them in their home-town movie theatres. In the Tinseltown version of Occupied Europe, the locals – the men

2

in berets and striped vests, the women in short skirts and revealing plenty of 'ooh-la-la!' cleavage – had desired nothing more fervently than to be freed from those jackbooted, black-uniformed sadistic swine who wore the evil crooked cross on their sleeves.

So the Yanks prepared for the great adventure: the liberation of a people who were going to be freed whether they liked it or not. They would bring with them their brass bands to play them ashore, waving their outsize 'old glory', and wearing their smart 'Class A' uniforms. Some of the regular army officers would bring with them sporting rifles to hunt exotic gazelles in the desert, perhaps even elephants. After all, North Africa was the 'dark continent', wasn't it? Real weapons they wouldn't need, of course. They were Americans after all, and everyone loved a Yank, didn't they? It was going to be roses, roses all the way.

Indeed, even before the 'Invasion' took place (if one could use such a bellicose term for the kind of operation the planners had conceived in Washington), the secret negotiations with the few French who seemed to support the plan turned out to be a bit of a farce. The senior American general was rumbled, the meeting place was raided by the gendarmes and the general escaped to the waiting British sub, only after losing his trousers in the surf.

Mind you, the future four-star general made the most of the absurd plight in which he had found himself. He turned the episode into a great personal adventure, his wife toured the USA giving speeches on the affair (and making good money doing so), and in the end the general who lost his pants had a permanent memorial erected to his great adventure – and the loss of his pants. It is still there in the United States as a symbol of US military glory. It includes the whole conning tower of the British submarine involved, which the general managed to secure and have dragged right across the States.[*]

Of course, in the end, as all these US 'liberation' missions have done in recent American military history, the farce turned into tragedy. Remember the first regular US troops landing in

[*]*HMS Seraph.*

Vietnam, with pretty local girls placing garlands of flowers around their necks? The French, who had not wanted to be liberated, fought back. In the first forty-eight hours of French resistance to the invaders, the Anglo-American liberators suffered 1,500 dead. The award of two Victoria Crosses to the British involved testified to the severity of the fighting.

After it was all over, Field Marshal Alexander could report to his political master, Winston Churchill, 'Sir, it is my duty to report . . . that the campaign is over. All enemy resistance has ceased. We are the masters of the North African shores.

But for how long? Yes, indeed, for just how long could the future masters of the Middle East, taking over the British role there, keep the peace?

Seven decades or so later, the great man who created what he believed was a 'special relationship' between Britain and 'our cousins over the seas', that same Winston Churchill, must be rotating madly in his grave . . .

D H York, Spring 2005

Prologue

Massacre at Mers-el-Kebir,

July 1940

'Here you are, sir,' the radio officer said urgently, 'the French signal. From Admiral Darlan to Admiral Gensoul.' He handed the decoded message to Admiral Somerville, the commander of the British Task Force H.

Hastily the middle-aged admiral put on his glasses. The commander of the Royal Navy's assault force anchored just off the French coast had been waiting for this signal for nearly forty-eight hours now. It was vital to know what kind of orders the new French government which had just surrendered to the Germans was giving to the French fleet commander who had fled before the victorious Germans to this North African port.

Somerville frowned as he skimmed the message. Tensely his captains waited for him to speak. They all knew what kind of decision the admiral might have to make. It was a terrible one. If he did nothing, the French Mediterranean fleet might well fall into the hands of the Germans. If he did order the attack, then they would be firing on men who had been their trusted allies only the month before. It was a decision that none would have liked to make.

Slowly Somerville looked up from the decoded message. His face was very solemn. He cleared his throat. 'This is what that devil Darlan has signalled, gentlemen.' For a moment he stared around at the faces of his captains as if he were seeing them for the very first time. Then he read them the message. 'Whatever orders are received, Gensoul, never surrender your ships intact. If they are attacked by either the Germans or the English, go and fight, or scuttle them. Signed – Darlan.'

Slowly, as if he hardly realized he was doing so, he let the signal drop. The others watched it flutter down to the deck. There was something very final about the gesture.

For a moment there was a heavy silence in the *Hood*'s wardroom, as Somerville's captains took in the full impact of the signal. Outside, a petty officer was snapping, 'Look lively, me lucky lads! You're gonna earn yer pay this day, I'll be bound.'

Somerville frowned at the petty officer's words. He cleared his throat and said, 'You all know Darlan. He hates the English. They say he has never got over the French Navy's defeat at Trafalgar. Now that he's hand in glove with the Huns, he'll do everything in his power to harm Britain, and especially the Royal Navy. That message, gentlemen, is not aimed at the Huns, but at us.'

There was a murmur of agreement from the assembled officers, but it was only half-hearted. Somerville was not a particularly sensitive or perceptive man, but he knew that most of his officers didn't agree with the course he would soon be forced to take.

'But we can't simply tackle the French like that, sir,' one of the captains voiced their reaction. 'Why, sir, they were our allies, fighting side by side with us, up to last month. It wouldn't be cricket to have a crack at them just like that . . .' His words trailed away to nothing and his weather-beaten face flushed a deeper red, as if he were abruptly embarrassed.

'I know, Connors, I know,' Somerville attempted to soothe the speaker. 'But unfortunately war isn't cricket. Let the French fleet over there continue to exist intact and, one, it would probably mean we'd lose control of the Med; and, two, sooner or later the Hun will seize those ships, most of them more modern than our own, and use them against us, even if they have to man them with German crews.'

But Captain Connors wasn't going to be silenced so easily. 'I understand,' he said, face flushing an ever deeper red. 'But can't we give them a last chance before we have to—' He broke off suddenly. It was as if he dare not even mention the final alternative.

Somerville turned to Captain Holland, who had once been the naval attaché in Paris and who spoke fluent French. 'Well, what do you think of that, Holland?' he asked, but before the commander of the aircraft carrier *Ark Royal* could reply, he added hurriedly, 'But first let me tell you Mr Churchill's attitude.' He put on his glasses once again and snapped, 'I received this signal from the PM only an hour ago. Here it is.' In the case of a French refusal to obey our instructions and surrender their ships to you or to sail them to a neutral port, it is the firm intention of HM Government to destroy them forthwith. WSC.' He looked directly at Captain Holland.

'Sir,' Holland replied immediately, 'I am not in favour of an attack, if that is the plan. There is still a chance that Admiral Gensoul –' he meant the commander of the French fleet – 'might still listen to reason, despite Darlan. He's a reasonable man and not anti-British like Darlan—'

'Cor, ferk a duck!' the petty officer's voice cut into Captain Holland's words. 'Look at them Frenchies, will yer, lads. They're getting up steam. They're gonna do a bunk or something.'

As one, the assembled officers stared through the great open port of the wardroom. Some mile or so away, silhouetted against the bright lights of the port, they could see the smoke beginning to drift from the stacks of some of the French ships. Connors said excitedly, 'That's the *Strasbourg* and Admiral Gensoul's flagship, the *Dunkerque*, they're both raising steam.'

'Yes,' another captain chimed in, 'and they're clearing the deck of that destroyer over there. It looks as if their matelots are tossing gear over the side into the harbour, they're in that much of a hurry.'

Somerville bit his bottom lip. Next to him, Captain Holland looked very worried. They both knew what this sudden activity in the French fleet at Mers-el-Kebir meant. But it was the plaintive Yorkshire voice of some unknown rating under the command of the loud-mouthed petty officer who put their dire thoughts into words. 'Well, I'll go to our house,' the Yorkshireman exclaimed. 'Yon froggie buggers are gonna have a bash . . . *They're ruddy well gonna fight!*'

Somerville would never forget those first moments of the cruel slaughter of the French fleet and their crews. He was up on the bridge of the *Hood* with his staff, where they had a clear all-round view of the French ships making a desperate attempt to slip their cables and open fire. In the dead silence, one that could almost be felt, he heard the measured voices of the gun controllers putting the guns on their targets. Slowly and steadily the *Hood*'s great triple cannon swung round. Up in the director's tower behind the bridge, the calm voice of the officer in charge said, 'Director layer sees the target.' That meant the guns were ready to fire and his finger was itching on the trigger. The French ships were at a range of not more than four thousand yards. Point-blank.

Somerville started, although he was expecting the noise. It was the *ping-ping* of the firing gongs. A great orange flash. A violent shudder. The six forward guns burst into angry noise simultaneously. A noise like an express train roaring through an empty midnight station at top speed. The huge shells sped towards their target. They couldn't miss.

The battleship the *Bretagne* was hit first. A shell slammed into the ammunition of her after turret. Another exploded in her after engine room. Flame seared the sky like an enormous blowtorch. Within minutes half the battleship was afire as two further shells struck the dying ship. Black mushrooms of thick smoke shot to the sky. She began to sink immediately, taking a thousand men of her crew, trapped at their stations, with her.

Somerville shook his head in despair. For a moment he shaded his eyes with his hand as if he might be trying to hide tears. But there was no room for sentiment now. The French began to retaliate. The French *Provence* had managed to move some distance from the quay when she fired two salvoes at Somerville's flag-ship, the *Hood*. Little damage was done, but the fleet gunnery officer was not going to tolerate the French firing back. His guns turned their attention to the *Provence* immediately.

The French ship reeled alarmingly as she was struck in the after turret. The ammunition locker was penetrated. The shells started to burn. Here and there they zig-zagged crazily into the sky. The *Provence* was hit again. She slumped to one side. Desperately, her skipper fought to keep his ship afloat as she headed back to the shore, taking water all the time. Just in time, before she sank altogether she ran aground, with her sailors fleeing over the side, swimming frantically for safety.

8

Now the British ships pounded the trapped French relentlessly. The latter hadn't a chance of escaping now. The destroyer *Mogador* had her stern blown off. A blazing wreck, she was towed back to the harbour by another destroyer which had attempted to escape with her.

Watching in fascinated horror from the bridge, Somerville knew the French were going to be wiped out if they didn't surrender soon. Whole turrets and a mass of debris flew through the blazing sky. The ships themselves were glowing torches, on fire from end to end. Everywhere there were shouting, frantic men in the water, struggling to survive, as chunks of razor-sharp, red-hot debris rained down on them. 'God in heaven!' Somerville moaned to himself. 'Surrender, will you . . . For God's sake, Gensoul, I beg you – *surrender*!' But still the merciless slaughter went on . . .

Captain Mercier of French Naval Intelligence, focused his glasses on the terrible scene below. Now the sea off the quay was packed with dead men and debris floating in a film of oil. On the crowded quay itself, trembling survivors were being pushed to and fro by giant Senegalese of the Colonial Infantry, intent on looting the naval stores. Here and there their white officers attempted to stop them, firing their pistols into the air wildly. But the great black soldiers in their tarboosh caps, sweat-shining, scarred faces eager for loot, were out of control. Some were already drunk. Others were threatening the officers with their long, old-fashioned bayonets. All was chaos, confusion and sudden, violent death.

'*Sales cons – les anglais,*' Mercier cursed. He lowered his glasses. He couldn't bear to see any more. His trapped comrades were being massacred. They hadn't stood a chance. The English swine stood between them and the open sea. Once they had raised steam and were about to sail, the English hadn't hesitated a moment. It had been the signal for the *Rosbifs* to open fire. What had happened next hadn't been war; it had been sheer bloody murder.

Down below, the ships' flags were hoisted. Here and there the surviving ships were raising their guns high into the air or draping their superstructure with white sheets to indicate that they would fight no more; that they were beaten. Those which

9

had survived that merciless bombardment at close range were ready to surrender.

Mercier slammed his gold-braided white cap squarely on his shaven head, strapped on his pistol and strode out of the office. He pushed a tall Senegalese, who was drinking straight from a litre bottle of *rouge*, to one side. The black soldier staggered back and was about to curse the officer when he saw the pistol in Mercier's hand. '*Pardon, M'sieu l'officier,*' he mumbled, red wine spilling down the front of his tunic.

'*Cochon!*' Mercier snapped and strode on.

From the Bar de la Legion, he could hear the Germans of the Foreign Legion singing their marching hymn, '*Tiens, voilà du boudin, voilà du boudin pour les Alsaciens, les Suisses et les Lorrains . . . pour les Belges, il n'y en a plus . . .*'

Mercier didn't hesitate. He knew that they were Germans and probably drunk by this time too; you could always rely on the Legion, especially if there was the chance of a fight. He shouted, '*A moi la Legion! . . . Vite . . . à moi la Legion . . .*'

As if they had been waiting for just this order all the time, the shaven-headed, hardbitten Legionnaires poured from their bar, slamming on their white kepis, some brandishing naked bayonets, others pulling on knuckledusters. They skidded to a stop when they saw a red-faced angry Mercier standing there, a drawn pistol in his hand, glaring at the drunken black infantry, who were making France's disgrace even worse by this looting and breakdown of discipline. '*Caporal,*' he addressed a giant of a Legionnaire with a nasty scar running down the side of his pock-marked face. 'Your name?'

Drunk as he was, the big corporal snapped to attention, arms stretched stiffly down the side of his white drill uniform. 'Hartmann,' he barked. 'Hartmann, Hans.'

'*Gut, Hartmann, Hans,*' Mercier cried in German. '*Sie haben das Kommando . . .* Clear away this disgraceful black mob.'

The corporal didn't hesitate. '*Jawohl, Herr Kapitan!*' he snapped. He turned to the others. '*Los, Jungs!*' he bellowed above the racket made by the dying fleet and the cries of the drunken Senegalese, who were now beginning to break into

10

the shops on the quayside. *'Mir nach. Jetzt gibt's remmidemmi!'*

The Legionnaires needed no urging. They waded into the black infantry at once. They caught the Senegalese, half drunk as most of them were, by complete surprise. Most of them were armed. But they didn't get a chance to use their rifles or bayonets. The Legionnaires were too quick for them. Using their boots, knuckledusters and brass-bound belts wrapped around their fists, yelling at the tops of their voices in German, they threw the black infantry back.

Captain Mercier now ignored the fighting men. The Germans would take care of that particular problem for him. Now he concentrated on the burning fleet and the wretched survivors, who might have a chance once the ambulances from Oran arrived.

Some of the sailors who had managed to reach the quayside were in a pitiful state. In front lay a young sailor, naked except for his sailor cap, the *pompon rouge*. He lay on his back, gasping out the last moments of his life, vomiting blood mixed with thick black diesel oil. Next to him lay another survivor. He was already dead. He had lived only minutes after someone had dragged him out of the water with what appeared to have been a boat hook. Now he lay there, his upper body charred a crusty black, his wounds a startling scarlet where the flesh had burst in the intense heat of his burning ship. Beyond him a young midshipman, who looked barely seventeen, was rocking back and forth on his knees, his hands clasped together, as if he were praying. For what, Mercier didn't know. His upper face looked as if someone had thrown a handful of strawberry jam at it. His eyes had gone, too. Where they had been were now two pink suppurating pits from which an evil-looking fluid leaked. 'Shoot me,' he croaked abruptly. 'Please, in God's name – *shoot me!*'

A little way off a tough old petty officer, minus his right arm, cried, 'Kids, just off their mother's tit . . . *Cochonerie! Sale cochonerie!* Knock it off, kid . . . What do you think this is – a fucking finishing school for high-born young ladies—' He keeled over abruptly, the curse dying in his throat as he fell to the cobbles, dead or unconscious before he hit them.

11

Hot vomit filled Mercier's mouth. He fought against the urge to be sick. Instead he turned away from the sight of such misery. The *Rosbifs* had gone now. They had done their dirty work. They had betrayed France. They had slaughtered her seamen ruthlessly in cold blood without giving them a chance to fight back. But it had been typical of the English; it had been always thus. Abruptly his feeling of sadness and nausea was replaced by one of burning rage. He raised his clenched fist and shook it at that darkening horizon where the *Rosbifs* were. '*Damn you, Englishmen . . . and damn you again . . . One day you will pay for what you have done here!*'

Book One

Journey into Fear

'History with its flickering lamp stumbles along the trail of the past trying to reconstruct its success, to revive the echoes and kindle with pale gleams the passions of former days.'

Winston Churchill

One

Lieutenant Horatio Smythe pushed his way through the happy, jostling crowd emerging from the grounds of Buckingham Palace, skirting the ruins left by the German bomber attack of 1940, two years before. Now the band of the Guards had ceased playing and the investiture was over. The crowd was relaxing, having their photos taken by smiling relatives. Some of the recipients of honours were in pre-war formal dress, complete with top hats and frock coats. They were the civil servants who would now proudly add 'OBE' and 'MBE' after their names on the office stationery. But most of them were in service dress, with a surprising number of 'other ranks' among them, keenly watched by the eagle eyes of the Guards sergeant majors, who strode back and forth near the Palace gates, their pacing sticks beneath their arms.

Smythe gave a sigh of relief that the ceremony was over. Somewhat furtively he removed the DSC medal from his naval tunic and put it into its case and into his pocket. He threaded his way through the silly gushing women in their large pre-war hats and smelly old fur tippets and was grateful for the fact that he had not told his mother that he was going up to the palace to receive his gong for bravery on the 'Murmansk Run'*. Mummy would have been just as gushing and as silly as these women, proud of her darling boy.

The nervous, sick King-Emperor had been very kind. He'd even asked about what he was going to do now that he'd lost his ship on the dangerous run to Russia, and had stuttered, 'I

*See: Duncan Harding, *Convoy of Death* (Severn House) for further details.

15

am s–sure you are the youngest present today Smythe . . . G–good luck to you.'

Still, the question had raised again the dangerous and depressing thought of what would be his next posting. What was left of the old 'Mucky Duck' as the crew had called his last one, the minesweeper HMS *Black Swan,* had been scrapped, and the surviving members of her crew paid off. Now, with the damned medal he had been awarded, it was more than likely he might be posted to some enormous battle wagon to hold down some executive job up at Scapa Flow. After the dangerous adventures of that 'Murmansk Run', he didn't think he could stand the boring routine of that kind of posting.

He stopped momentarily as a company of Home Guard marched past with a smart 'eyes right' for the Palace. The old boys were doing their best, their chests thrown out proudly, especially as some of the newly arrived Yanks were snapping their photos, presumably for the 'folks back home'. Smythe forced a smile for the portly company commander, chest bright with four rows of medal ribbons, his white 'tea-strainer moustache', probably dating from the Boer War, waxed and stiff.

But once he had passed, the young officer's smile vanished. He couldn't see the old boys doing much to finish off Hitler in this year of '42; nor their new ally, the Yanks, either. Even to his youthful eye, the Americans, who had been Britain's ally since Pearl Harbor, seemed to be very green, very unsol-dierly, with their hands in their pockets or lounging at street corners, chewing their gum like cows chewing their cud.

Back at Haslar, where they'd looked him over and checked that his minor wounds from the Murmansk Run had healed so that he could be classified as fit for active service once more, the doctor who had examined him had said, 'Now then, young Smythe, go back to London and enjoy yourself for a couple of days. Pick yourself up some lady of the night round Shaftesbury Avenue way. If you take sensible precautions, you'll get nothing worse than a case of bad breath and sudden lightening of your wallet.' The middle-aged doctor had laughed and added, 'This is going to be a long war, Smythe, and God knows what will happen to young fellers like yourself. Enjoy yourself while you . . . Carpe diem and all that, you know.' The doctor had smiled and, just like the King-Emperor a few moments ago, he had ended with 'good luck to you'. If he had been a more imaginative youth, Smythe might have thought that both of them, the doctor and the King, weren't expecting him to survive very long.

Now the young, fresh-faced naval lieutenant sighed and wondered how he might take the Haslar doctor's advice and enjoy life while he still had a chance to do so. He had never been alone in the capital before and he had certainly never picked up a woman, especially a whore. How did one go about doing so? He was well prepared. His pocket bulged with his back pay and he had a pack of six 'French letters', as the matelots called them, though he'd never tried a contraceptive on before. How did one go about it, while playing with – hopefully – a woman's things? Perhaps the woman, if she were a whore, would do it for him? On the old 'Mucky Duck', the ratings had always been rabbiting on about what they had done to women and what women – 'tarts', as they called them – had done for them. It had seemed so easy for them as he had listened, shy and red-faced, to the tales of their sexual exploits. But perhaps that was because they were lower-deck and working-class. The matelots were more carefree and easy-going than people of his own class. He sighed once again. What *was* he going to do? He hesitated, wondering whether he should turn left or right, and what difference it would make either way.

'Fancy a bit, sailor?' The query, in the ripest cockney, cut right into his somewhat bewildered reverie. He swung round, taken completely off guard, expecting to be faced by some undersized London spiv on the make.

To his surprise, he was not confronted by some cockney spiv, but by a naval lieutenant-commander, dressed in an immaculate uniform, which might well have come from some fancy bespoke tailor in Saville Row. Smythe straightened to attention immediately and automatically his Dartmouth training clicked in and he said loudly, 'Good afternoon, sir. Can I help you?'

The big commander with the merry eyes and broken nose said, 'Please relax, Smythe. You've had a hard time since you left the college. Now you must learn to relax and enjoy yourself.'

Smythe told himself that this was the third person in authority who had seemed to be concerned about his personal welfare in the last three days or so; it was almost embarrassing. Aloud he said, 'Thank you, sir. But have I done anything wrong, sir?'

The commander clapped him on the shoulder in an avuncular fashion. 'Of course not, my boy. We've just been keeping an eye on you and we like what we see. A DSC before you're even twenty, and taking over the command of that old tub of yours between Murmansk and the knackers' yard. Excellent work for a snotty kid just out of Dartmouth. But come on, my boy. Let's have a pink gin and a bit of a talk, eh?'

Without waiting for an answer, he put his arm around Smythe and steered him towards the line of taxis waiting to take the people from the palace back to their railway stations. Standing nearby, the newspaper vendor paused in his hoarse cries of, 'Bremen attacked agen . . . Nazis lose twenty planes . . . read all about it,' to murmur, 'Bloody pansies. The Navy's full of the friggers . . .'

The private drinking club located in a cellar just off Shaftesbury Avenue was packed with officers of all three services, and spivs and cheap-looking peroxide blondes, both with calculating, knowing eyes. All seemed to Smythe half drunk despite the earliness of the hour, and all were obviously animated by the sale of sex for money. Elderly waiters in rusty old pre-war tailcoats hurried back and forth, carrying silver trays of black-market drinks. Helping them were plump brassy waitresses, whose bottoms were routinely pinched by the red-faced servicemen, although the women could have been the mothers of most of the men present. Everywhere there hung blue clouds of cigarette smoke that made the patrons cough and choke. Not that it mattered. They were too excited to care. Besides, most of them were fated to die sooner or later and they were enjoying this time out of the war, and comfort from the knowledge that the bought women would provide before the day was out.

'A high-priced knocking shop really, Smythe,' said the commander, who still hadn't given the bewildered younger officer his name. 'But it's a place where a chap can relax and get a decent drink at this time of the day. Besides, it's so bloody noisy,' he added, 'that even your closest neighbour at the next table can't hear what you're saying.' He winked knowingly. 'And we don't want that, do we, eh?'

'No sir,' Smythe replied, not knowing what else to say.

The strange commander clicked his fingers and now Smythe noticed that two of them were missing. Immediately the patron, who had been busy at the bar with a flashy-looking civilian who looked particularly well-fed and prosperous and who was probably a large-scale black marketeer, turned. A large smile appeared at once on his greasy face and he pushed his way through the throng to where the commander waited. He shook the naval officer's hand warmly, looked a little dubiously at Smythe, and then inclined his head, shining with brilliantine, at the two women at the far end of the bar. They were smoking through cigarette holders and were showing more than enough silk-clad leg. Smythe's heart quickened at the sight. He could imagine running his hand up those stockings to find the source of all delight above. He swallowed hard.

The commander shook his head. 'Not today, Angelo, thank you. Just two pink gins – large, of course – for the moment.'

'Angelo' looked shocked. He rolled his dark eyes. 'Pink gins, *Signor Commandante*!' he exclaimed, raising his podgy hands aloft as if the naval officer was demanding the Holy Grail itself. But in due course he appeared, beaming and bearing the drinks on a silver tray, guarding it with his elbow, as if he feared someone might bump into him and upset the precious gift. 'The last,' he whispered. 'For you personally, *Commandante*.'

The commander wasn't impressed. 'We'll take a pew here, Angelo, and when I give the signal, keep 'em coming, would you . . . And be a good chap, remember – *large*.'

With that he ignored the patron and, raising his glass in toast, said, 'Here's to your gong. You certainly deserve it.' They drank and he continued, with, 'Now, young feller, let's have a bit of a chinwag, what. How do you feel about subs?'

The question caught Smythe completely off guard. 'Subs, sir?' he echoed somewhat foolishly.

'Yes, you've been in one, I suppose?'

'Yessir, at Dartmouth we did the short sub course.'

'No claustrophobia – anything like that?'

'No sir.'

'Good show!' The Commander downed his pink gin in one large swallow and signalled to Angelo, who pretended to be a Maltese, but who was in reality an Italian and in theory, at least, an enemy alien who should have been interned.

'*Porco di Madonna!*' the patron cursed. His precious supply of pink gin was diminishing rapidly, but the *Commandante* was not a man to be crossed. He was a man who could cause trouble for anyone who did so, and Angelo didn't want trouble. So, reluctantly, he poured out another generous couple of glasses of the black-market gin.

'Now you're wondering why I singled you out, Smythe, and why I asked what must appear to be damned fool questions, eh?'

The latter thought it wiser not to answer.

'Well, I'll tell you, Smythe. You're a brave fellow and you've handled a craft under fire and, to be frank, there are not too many officers of your calibre available. We need every officer we can find for the Atlantic crossings now that the Yanks are coming over in large numbers to protect the troop-ships. So their Lordships –' he meant the Admiralty – 'have allowed us to have you – for a time . . .' He lowered his voice slightly. 'For a hush-hush op.'

Suddenly Smythe felt a sense of excitement. 'What kind of hush-hush op?'

'Just tell me you're prepared to accept, then I'll give you a clue.'

'Of course I am prepared, sir. I'll do anything I can to help, sir.'

'Well said, young feller.'

'Now this is the drill. You are to report to flag officer Portsmouth. Pompey'll give you the information you need for starters. As soon as Bill Jewell comes back from his latest mission, he'll brief you further.' He paused as a drunken US

20

captain staggered up to the place's piano, his arm round an equally drunken blonde whose breasts were threatening to burst out of a tight silken blouse at any moment, and then asked swiftly, 'Oh, by the way, do you like our new allies, the Yanks?'

But before a now completely bewildered Smythe could answer that particular question, the American had slumped on the piano stool, placed the giggling blonde on his knee and had started hammering out, bellowing the words as he did so, *'Over there . . . over there . . . have a care, for the Yanks are coming . . . over there . . .'*

Two

Scarlet flame stabbed the darkness. A bullet howled off the shingle only a couple of feet away from where the landing party crouched, waiting for their dinghies. Another flare sailed into the night sky. *Crack!* It exploded in a burst of brilliant silver light.

Some hundred yards away, on the conning tower of HMS *Seraph*, the submarine's skipper focused his night glasses and cursed at what he saw. The Germans were attempting to come in from both flanks in order to cut off the SBS* commandos who had taken the French agents ashore, and they were covered by a Spandau, firing a thousand rounds a minute from the heights beyond. The slugs seemed to be hitting all around the trapped men in a solid stream of lethal morse.

Still the SBS waiting for the rubber boats to take them back to the British submarine were holding the German attackers off. They knew their fate if the Germans captured them alive. They'd be tortured to make them reveal what they knew of the local French resistance, before being shot without trial under Hitler's new 'Commando Order'.

Commander Jewell swept the sea with his glasses. There were the two dinghies manned by his own ratings. They were making slow progress in the heavy sea just off the shore. Time and time again, the waves drove them back from the beach and they were being forced to paddle all out just to keep from capsizing. He cursed again, telling himself that if he didn't do something quick, the five SBS would be overrun and that would be that. Not only that, it wouldn't be long before the Germans spotted the submarine just off shore. Then the sub

*Special Boat Service, the naval equivalent of the SAS.

chasers would be swarming out of nearby Lorient eager for the kill.

Hastily he made his decision. He bent over the voice tube. 'Engine room, stand by for immediate action,' he commanded, shouting now above the frenetic, hysterical fury of the German machine gun firing all out. 'Gun crew topside . . . at the double . . . man your piece . . .'

There was a clatter of boots on the ladder that led from the red glow of the sub's interior to the conning tower. Next moment the gun crew were pushing back-to-back past Jewell and doubling along the wet deck of the submarine towards the bow quick-firer. They went into action immediately. With a dull thump, the shell tore from the gun, the casing clattering to the deck.

Jewell groaned. The shell exploded beyond the machine gun. For a moment the Germans ceased firing, then the Spandau spat white death once more and the infantry began attacking again, crying wildly as if they were drunk or drugged, or both.

'For God's sake, get your finger out, chaps!' a desperate Jewell yelled above the snap-and-crack of small-arms fire. 'They'll have had it in half a mo!'

Still the handful of SBS men kept on returning fire bravely and the best they could, while the ratings in the dinghies fought the angry white surf.

Then the invaders' luck turned. The quick-firer belched fire once more. This time the gunners' aim was true. As the Germans fired another flare, illuminating that desperate scene of bloody action in its unreal white, glowing light, their shell struck home. The Spandau erupted in violent flame. Screaming and shrieking, its crew flew to both sides, a mess of bloody flailing limbs. Jewell yelled his approval. Next moment, he cried down the voice tube. 'Engine room – both astern!'

The engine-room artificers reacted at once. They knew just how dangerous their position was. The German E-boats might well be on their way to trap them before they could submerge and seek the safety of the bottom of the sea. With a belch, a stink of diesel, the engines pulsated with full power. The rudder churned the shallow water off the beach into a boiling white fury. Immediately the men in the dinghies felt themselves swept forward with the water.

Now other ratings from the off-duty watch came tumbling up the ladder from below to commence opening fire with their rifles. The Germans went down everywhere. Again the quick-firer joined in, forcing the other Germans attempting to come down from the fortified heights to go to ground. Jewell grabbed his loudhailer. He turned on the power and yelled at the top his voice, 'Run for it, lads . . . at the double now . . . There's no time to be wasted!'

The SBS men needed no urging. They rose from their hiding place. Backing towards the beach, they fired sharp short bursts from their sten guns to left and right, trying to keep the Germans at bay till they reached the dinghies, which were being swept in at a fast rate now by the artificial tide caused by the submarine's screws.

Five minutes later they were clambering into the wildly swaying rubber craft, dragging a wounded comrade with them, and the ratings were paddling back to the waiting submarine with all their strength as the frustrated Germans rushed the shore and started firing furiously at the escapees . . .

'Sir.'

'Yes?' Jewell put his cup of hot cocoa down and turned to the pale-faced hydrophone operator who had slipped off one of his earphones. 'Where's the fire?'

'Surface contact . . . bearing green-eight-five, sir.'

'Size?' Jewell snapped urgently.

'Large, sir . . . looks like several craft.'

'Great balls of fire!' Jewell cursed angrily. 'The buggers are on to us earlier than I thought.' He turned to his second-in-command. 'Up periscope – surface height . . . We'll have a look see, eh, Number One.'

'Sir!' The younger officer pressed the button. There was a hiss of compressed air. The shining steel tube of the periscope shot upwards to the usual thirty-five feet or so, where it would probably just break the surface of the sea.

Jewell wasted no time. He thrust his battered cap round so that the peak was to the back of his head. Then he went down on his knees so that he wouldn't need to raise the periscope much further. Cautiously he spun the scope round. At 180 degrees he spotted the dark shapes heading towards them. He turned up the enhancer. The craft shot into sharper focus. 'E-boats,' he announced for the sake of the duty watch, who were waiting tensely for his verdict. 'Jerries all right.'

Now he could see the sharp-prowed, sleek craft quite clearly. They had a white bone in their teeth, as if they were heading for the beach the *Seraph* had left only minutes before at top speed.

'Down periscope,' he ordered and, straightening up, he added, 'They're on to us, lads. Silent running. Hydrophone operator, keep us in the picture.'

'Sir.'

Now the normal lighting of the submarine was dimmed to a blood-red. The men of the duty watch moved softly, if they moved at all. In the bunks, where the off-duty men 'hot-bunked' in the beds just vacated by their comrades of the duty watch, the snorers had their mouths closed forcibly. Everything was suddenly tense, strained and silent as the hydrophone operator, white-faced and grim, listened to pick up the first sound of any E-boat coming into the area above them. Standing next to the periscope, Jewell, old hand that he was, felt a nerve on the left side of his face begin to tick with almost unbearable tension.

'Enemy approach,' the operator whispered, the beads of sweat beginning to trickle down his face.

Jewell nodded. He could already hear the thud-thud of the approaching craft's screws. He felt his hands tighten to stiff claws. He ordered himself to relax. He did so. Moments later, he found his hands tightening again.

'*Ping . . . ping.*' A sound like gravel being scattered along the hull of the *Seraph*. He knew what it was. Above, the German E-boat was bouncing the asdic detector off the hull. Around him the crew were suddenly white-faced, their singlets black with sweat. They all knew what might well be coming their way in a few moments if they were unlucky. A series of depth charges, which could well end their young lives before they had really begun to live.

'Steady, lads!' Jewell snapped, and fell silent immediately,

25

as the ping-ping of the asdic ended and the noise of the enemy craft's screws grew fainter and fainter and then vanished altogether. He breathed a sigh of relief. Around him most of the crew did the same. O'Rourke, the Catholic 'deserter' from the Irish Republic's tiny navy, kissed his rosary beads as if they had already saved him and smiled at the skipper. Jewell held his finger to his lips for the red-headed Irishman not to speak. They weren't out of danger yet. The German Navy didn't usually give up that easily.

The young skipper was right. At the hydrophone, the operator started abruptly. He pressed the earphones tighter to his ears, holding his breath as he tried to pick up the sound. Or had he imagined it? He hadn't.

Faintly, but getting ever stronger, he could hear the thud-thud of a ship's propellers once again. 'They're coming back, sir,' he announced.

'Thank you,' Jewell answered in the calmest voice he could muster. He knew from experience that it was only the submarine skipper who could keep the crew calm in such situations. He must not betray the slightest sign of worry or fear when things got dicey. That would be fatal. He pretended to stare at his dirty nails, as if he were bored, while the eyes of the crew flashed from his face to that of the hydrophone operator, which was greased with sweat once more.

The noise of the props grew louder and louder. Now the enemy craft was directly above them. There was the ping of the electronic waves bouncing off the hull. Jewell stopped looking at his nails. The Jerries had spotted them this time. How could they not find the old *Seraph* when they were right above the sub, the two of them separated by no more than a score of fathoms of water.

He was right. Abruptly the ping-ping of the asdic ceased. The crew tensed. O'Rourke, the Irishman, tried to ease the tension. 'For what we are about to receive,' he intoned in a funereal voice, 'may the Good Lord make us truly thankful . . .'

'Put a sock in it, O'Rourke,' Jewell snapped. 'I—' But he never finished the sentence.

There was a hollow boom like some giant striking the sub's hull with a massive steel hammer. A depth charge exploded

26

to port. The submarine rocked alarmingly. Hastily the men grabbed for stanchions and shelves for support. Next moment another depth charge followed, closer this time. Here and there, tough glass dials splintered.

Jewell knew what the Germans were up to. He had been through this kind of misery before. They were dropping a pattern to port and starboard, moving ever closer to the *Seraph*'s hull. Naturally they hoped that one of their 'water bombs', as they called the depth charges in their own language, might score a direct hit on the submarine. But anything that exploded close to her might do the trick, too. Once the *Seraph* sprang a serious leak and the sea water ran into the submarine's electric batteries, all hell would be let loose. Choking gas would develop and their air wouldn't last long. One lucky hit like that and the Germans knew the English submariners would never see daylight again.

Thus the long ordeal of HMS *Seraph* commenced . . .

Three

'*Bless 'em all, the long and the short and the tall,*' the old sailor sang moodily as he chipped away at the rust on the little ship's hull. *Bless all the corporals and their bleeding sons . . .*' Not far off an old civilian fisherman was gutting his catch. Hurtling themselves at the scraps, the gulls came streaming like dive bombers. It could have been a perfect scene, the sort of thing Smythe remembered from holidays in Cornwall, save for one thing: the lean grey deadly shapes of the submarines anchored out across from Portsmouth 'Hard'.

Reluctantly the old sailor stood up and touched his horny hand to his cap. 'Morning, sir,' he said.

Smythe thought that the rating had given him a decidedly sloppy salute and deserved a reprimand, but he had not the heart to do so. His mind was full of other things. 'Morning,' he said instead and, nodding out to the submarine flotilla, said, 'No sign of HMS *Seraph*, I suppose?'

'No sir,' the old sailor said. 'But not to worry, sir. Commander Jewell, he's like a ruddy moggy – he's got nine lives that officer, sir.' The old sailor took up his rasp again and started scraping at the rust once more, as if he might well spend the rest of his life thus. The little interview was over. Smythe hesitated and then he set off once more, while the old sailor began his mournful chant about the soldiers – 'time-expired and bound for the land they adore' – ending with a slight alteration to the original chorus, changing it to, 'You'll get no promotion this side of the ocean, so cheer up my lads, fuck 'em all . . .'

Smythe grinned briefly and, for a moment or two as he walked, staring at empty grey sea, he shared the same nihilistic sentiment. He had been in Portsmouth two days now. He had been received immediately by the flag captain in charge so he knew that whatever Intelligence intended for him, it was a mission of some importance. Why else the instant reception by a senior four-ringer like the flag captain?

The older man had shaken his hand very firmly, as if testing the strength of his grip, and had barked, as if he were back on the quarterdeck of the cruiser he had once skippered, 'Welcome aboard, Smythe!' He had glanced at the single ribbon on Smythe's chest. 'I hear you won a good gong, young man. That's the kind of chap I think we'll need for this job. Good show.'

Smythe had stuttered something, trying not to flush in his usual embarrassed fashion when he was praised, and then had waited for the captain to tell him why he had been summoned to the naval port in such a roundabout, mysterious fashion. He hadn't learnt much. Indeed what little the other man had told him had mystified and puzzled him even more. 'You are to be briefed by Lt Commander William Jewell – Bill to most people – of the Third Submarine Flotilla. Commander Jewell is currently on patrol but he is expected to arrive back at Pompey within the next twenty-four hours. In the meantime you are to have yourself kitted out to participate in Jewell's next mission, which will sail as soon as his submarine, the *Seraph*, has been re-victualled etc. Is that clear, Smythe?'

In fact it had not been clear at all. He had been preparing himself to dare ask a question when the stern-faced bluff senior officer barked, 'Now get yourself over to the stores and ask for whatever gear you'll need for the next patrol – and remember this, Smythe. This is a very important assignment indeed. Keep your lips –' he paused and glared at the younger officer from under his thick, bushy eyebrows, before adding – 'very firmly sealed. Is that understood?'

He had said he had. But at that particular moment he had been so completely confused that he doubted if some modern-day Mata Hari could have gotten anything out of him even if she had used all her exciting female charms.

It was clear that they knew about him at the 'stores', and that he was expected. For he wasn't given the usual stores rating for whatever they were now about to kit him out for.

Instead he was attended to by the old, white-haired chief petty officer in charge of the place. And it was clear that the old sailor (who might well have served with Nelson himself on HMS *Victory*, which lay opposite, he seemed that old) was in the know. He banished the ratings from the great echoing place before he said in a soft voice to ensure that no one could hear, 'Well, sir you'll need the usual submariner's gear: pullover, socks and the like. And of course a camouflage smock as well.'

'Camouflage smock!' Smythe had echoed, puzzled. 'Why a camouflage smock in a submarine?'

''Fraid I can't say,' the CPO had answered, suddenly avoiding Smythe's gaze, and so he had gone back to his quarters, carrying the pile of clothing topped with a camouflage smock of the type worn by paratroopers and commandos, more bewildered than ever.

That afternoon, he had begun to realize that something strange was going on with the Third Submarine Flotilla. There were too many 'buzzes' floating about the wardroom, with submarine skippers, heavily bearded and pale-faced, as if they hadn't seen the sun for a long time, slumped in the battered horsehair chairs, sipping pink gins, who lowered their voices immediately he came close to them and flashed him suspicious looks.

Naturally most of the submarines of the flotilla seemed to be carrying out normal fighting patrols, intent on sinking enemy ships in the Channel and the like. But more than once Smythe picked up talk of subs doing 'taxi-rank jobs . . . running them into the Frog coves . . . There's plenty of 'em, thank God, and the Huns can't guard them all . . . But the Frogs do love to gossip . . . They find 'em all in the end, or mine the approaches so we can't get in.' Smythe, as bewildered as he was, still didn't need a crystal ball to realize what this kind of hushed, secretive talk between the submariners meant. Some of the Third Flotilla's craft were employed in running French agents into their native country, using the tiny harbours and coves which, as he knew from Dartmouth's navigation lessons, dotted the isolated coast of South-West France.

That day Smythe began to wonder if the powers that be had some sort of similar mission planned for him and the still missing

Lt Commander Jewell. The thought of such clandestine derring-do excited his youthful mind; it might well be the same sort of stuff that Hollywood was showing in the studios' wartime movies. But at the same time the thought frightened him a little too. He expected to die for King and Country; he'd had that bred into him from the first day he had attended his prep school. 'All that red on the map' and a sense of duty to the 'King-Emperor' had become part and parcel of his young life. Now he realized that if he were caught in France in some sort of covert mission, his fate would be sealed. Whether he was in uniform or not, the Huns would put him up against the nearest wall and shoot him out of hand, and that was not how he visualized ending his young life. There was simply nothing heroic about it.

'Sir,' a soft female voice broke into the young officer's reverie. 'Lieutenant Smythe, sir.'

He turned, a little startled. A young Wren, her pretty face flushed a delightful red with the effort of running across the Hard, was waving a paper at him, her plump breasts trembling slightly under her smart navy-blue tunic.

'Yes?' he answered, blushing a little, as he always did in the presence of women, although his virginity had been taken by the eager Russian woman skipper when the shattered convoy had finally reached Murmansk.* 'What is it?'

'I've got two messages for you, sir,' the Wren gasped. She came to attention and saluted smartly, her bright blue eyes beneath the trim cap taking in the ribbon of the DSC which adorned his tunic.

Casually, in the manner of a much senior officer, he returned her salute, hoping that she might take him to be older than he really was, for he guessed she might only be eighteen herself, a year younger than he was. 'Where is it, Wren . . . ?'

'Wren Tidmus, sir. Here, sir.' She handed him the piece of paper she was carrying, still standing to attention so he had to order her, while he glanced at the requisition, 'Please stand at ease, Wren Tidmus.' He frowned. The paper stated he had permission to draw tropical kit from the stores. He looked up

*See: D. Harding, *Convoy of Death* (Severn House) for further details.

31

at the pretty Wren. 'But I only drew normal submarine gear forty-eight hours ago. Now this . . .' He paused and added, 'Do you understand it?'

She answered, 'No, I don't, sir. But sometimes, if I may say so between you and me, the powers that be do this for security reasons. One day it's Arctic gear. The next tropical.'

'Oh, I see,' he said. 'Thanks for the info. All right—'

He was about to tell her to go but she beat him to it, saying, 'The flag captain would like to speak to you, sir. Something has just come up concerning Commander Jewell. Would you like to follow me?'

'To the ends of the world,' Smythe heard himself saying, wondering at his new-found boldness with women, but then Wren Tidmus was really very pretty indeed.

The flag captain thanked the pretty Wren and then dismissed her to the next office, though Smythe had a feeling she was still watching as the captain closed the door and said, 'Well, we've heard from Bill – er, Commander Jewell. Indirectly, you understand?'

Smythe didn't, but then since he had arrived at Pompey he hadn't understood very much at all; every hour seemed to bring with it a new puzzle. He didn't tell the flag captain that, of course. He nodded his head and waited.

'Jewell's submarine is under attack . . . just off Brittany. Here.' He pointed a finger at a spot on the big map behind him, just below the German-held port of Lorient. 'One of our Coastal Command Sunderlands spotted an E-boat attack on the *Seraph* as the pilot was turning for home. His report has just come through. The pilot waited till he landed before he did so. He didn't want the Hun picking up his radio signal.'

Smythe felt constrained to say something, although he felt foolish as he stuttered, 'I'm sorry to hear . . . that, sir.'

'Not to worry, young man. Old Jerry'll have to get up earlier to catch Bill with his knickers down. He's been in worse scraps than this in the past. Commander Jewell is, in my opinion, a born survivor.'

'What's the drill now, sir?' Smythe heard himself saying, to say something, because he felt the other officer expected him to do so.

'Well,' the flag captain frowned and stroked his lantern jaw. 'He's a very experienced skipper, probably more experienced than the Huns attacking him. So he'll try the old tricks. You know, blow oil from a torpedo tube together with old seamen's duds, tins of food and the like, so that the Hun'll think a depth charge has hit the *Seraph* and she's sinking.' He stroked his chin harder. 'If that doesn't work, he'll lie low at the bottom of the sea, hoping he can outwait the Hun. In due course we'll send out a Sunderland from Coastal Command to try to frighten the Hun off. If that doesn't work, well, knowing Commander Jewell as I do, he just won't sit on this arse till it grows barnacles.' He laughed briefly at his own coarse humour. 'He'll surface while the crew's still got some oxygen left, and try to catch the Hun off guard. Then it'll be the one who gets off the first accurate shot who'll win.'

'And if that doesn't work, sir?' Smythe the innocent, who knew virtually nothing about submarine warfare, asked.

Abruptly the flag captain stopped stroking his chin. 'In the Third Submarine Flotilla, they don't even think about such things, Smythe,' he said severely. 'Negative thoughts are for losers, remember that, young man. Now then, dismiss!'

Feeling thoroughly deflated and put down in no uncertain terms, Smythe saluted the best he could and went through the door. Outside, the old sailor chipping rust off the ship's hull was still singing in his monotonous cracked voice about how *'you'll get no promotion this side of the ocean, so cheer up my lads – fuck 'em all . . .'*

At that particular moment a red-faced Smythe shared the sentiment . . .

Four

The Germans above the *Seraph* were echo-ranging again. It was two hours now since their last depth charge attack. Perhaps the enemy thought they had sunk the sub; why else should they echo-range instead of starting to drop another depth charge pattern?

Jewell paused in what he was doing and listened to the sonar signals and the *ping-ping* of the signal on the hull. If they were loud enough for the German operator to hear, he would be able to located the stationary submarine once again.

Jewell was not claustrophobic – he had never met anyone in the submarine service who was. All the same, those ominous pings had a strange impact on him. It was a sense of groping, a lonely feeling of being blind and unsafe because he couldn't see. Yet above them there was a dedicated enemy who could: a ship built to destroy subs – and a ship that was looking specifically for them.

He looked around the duty watch. The men's faces were glazed as if with vaseline and beads of sweat hung on their foreheads like opaque pearls. But there was no fear in their eyes as far as he could ascertain. But what would they look like in another couple of hours when their oxygen supply started to diminish rapidly? How steadfast would they be then? He dismissed that particulatly unpleasant thought. He had been through the final stages of oxygen deprivation before when he and the rest of another sub crew had been perhaps some twenty minutes or so away from death. He didn't want to go through that traumatic experience again.

He turned back to his number one. 'Stand by to fire,' he ordered. He had spoken very softly, as if the enemy might well be listening just outside the sub, with his ears pressed to the hull. But, in the heavy silence of the control room, everyone present heard him. Here and there men of the watch breathed a sigh of relief. Come what may now, but at least the long dread wait was over.

At the bow the torpedo outer doors swung open.

'Tubes one and two,' Jewell ordered in subdued voice again. The torpedo mates repeated the order.

Jewell nodded his satisfaction and then began to ease the boat upwards, fathom by fathom, head cocked to one side as he listened to that ominous *ping-ping*, which at any moment might prove their downfall.

Now, even before he had lined up their pursuer, Jewell made his decision – there would be no time for fancy plotting once the scope had broken the surface. He'd try for the enemy ship's starboard quarter, three-quarters of the way round from the bow. That would give him the largest possible target. With the back of his hand, he wiped the sudden sweat from his brow still aware of the enemy's sonar signals. Now there was a continuing cycle of louder and softer pings. That indicated that the Germans had not yet really spotted the *Seraph*. Instead they were scanning the area. All the same, Jewell knew they might pick him up at any second – and he didn't have a clue where the German craft was. This was certainly a a game of bloody blind man's bluff. He cursed. He was sweating again.

Five minutes passed. At the time it seemed like five years. They were almost at periscope height now. Should he chance it? He did. In a voice he could hardly recognize as his own, he ordered, 'Up periscope.'

A rush of compressed air. The shining tube rushed up. Hastily he flung himself behind it. He flashed a look through it. There she was – a large German E-boat of the latest class. But that was about all he had time to take in. In that same instant the ping-ping noise accelerated and he knew the *Seraph* had been located. 'Fire one and two!' he yelled, followed by 'Down scope!'

The sub shuddered as the first torpedo left her bow. An instant later, the second followed. At his side, his second-in-command glued his gaze to his stopwatch to time the run, his lips moving silently as he counted off the seconds. Jewell counted with him.

He had already estimated it would take less than thirty seconds to hit the target at that range. *'Twenty-eight . . . twenty-nine . . .'* He tensed for the explosion soon to come. *'Thirty . . .'* Nothing . . . *'Thirty-one . . .'* His whisper faltered away. They had missed, and now they were going to take some stick.

There was no time for 'silent running' now. The enemy craft would already have spotted them; the torpedoes had given them away. 'Flood negative!' he snapped, knowing that he'd have to make a run for it, chased by an enemy that could make thrice the speed he could with his slow electric motors.

Boom! the Germans had spotted the *Seraph* almost immediately. The sub shook and trembled like a live thing as the depth charge exploded close by.

Cork and paint chipped off the bulkheads. A glass dial splintered. Just over Jewell's head a lightbulb shattered. Rivets from the plates flew through the air like tiny bullets. Another click followed by a noise like some giant hitting the hull with a great sledgehammer, then the gushing sound of tons of water being displaced by the enemy depth charge. Next instant the submarine rocked crazily from side to side, with the men grabbing wildly for handholds.

Jewell wiped the blood from his face where he had struck a piece of machinery. He was scared – a little – but exhilarated too. His mind was racing electrically as he tried to outwit the German hunter.

He had already noted the rain squall on the horizon as he had shot a look through the periscope. Once they reached the rain squall, Jewell knew, they'd be in a much better position. There the enemy's sound equipment would be pretty useless for finding them. Besides, a rough-and-ready plan was beginning to unfurl in his mind like some deadly snake opening its coil ready to strike. Still, they had to reach the cover of the rain first.

Now their electric motors were going all out. Naturally he knew they couldn't outrun the surface craft with its superior speed. But if the *Seraph* could just reach the edge of the rain squall, Jewell knew they had a fighting chance of – his blue eyes gleamed at the prospect – giving the Jerry bastard a taste of his own medicine.

The *Seraph* lived up to her reputation in the Third Submarine Flotilla of being a lucky ship. As the matelots told it, 'Yon boat could fall in a shiteheap and come up smelling of attar of roses, mates.' Twice the hunter got within direct range and twice Jewell managed to dodge an accurate depth charge attack by changing course at the very last moment, with the *Seraph* reeling wildly under the impact of the depth charges exploding close by, but surviving.

Now Jewell guessed they must be approaching the edge of the squall. He could sense the turbulence in the water as the *Seraph* ploughed on desperately, her crew knowing that disaster could strike at any moment now. For even the most stupid crew member realized their luck couldn't hold out much longer. Jewell made his decision. '*Stand by aft tubes three and four*,' he ordered.

'*Close up three and four*,' the senior torpedo mate echoed.

Just behind them there came the thunder of the E-boat's screws. They could hear the churning noise made by the propellors quite clearly now. In a moment there'd come that dreaded click which would indicate that the German craft was about to drop another pattern of depth charges. And this time, Jewell knew, they wouldn't miss – they *couldn't* at that range – and that would be that for the old *Seraph*.

Jewell jutted his jaw hard. He was determined to escape. The old *Seraph* wouldn't go down without a fight. He thrust his upper body forward involuntarily, as if willing the submarine to reach the cover of the squall before the hunter caught up with her. It seemed the engine artificers sensed his urgent mood. They fussed and tinkered with the myriad tiny pistons of the sub's engines, listening to their workings with a kind of antiquated hearing aid, rubbing them clean of too much lubricating oil, faces wet with sweat, singlets black with perspiration, as if they were trying to get every last bit of power out of the electric motors.

Behind them the noise of the E-boat's screws became ever louder. Jewell knew it could be only a matter of minutes now before the enemy craft caught up with them. He grabbed the voice tube. 'Torpedo room!' he cried, noting just how hoarse his voice was with suppressed tension now. 'Prepare to fire!' he ordered.

Dutifully, Sandy Ferguson, the torpedo mate, echoed the order. Tough old twenty-year man that he was, his voice clearly revealed the strain he was under, too.

Suddenly the *Seraph* rocked wildly. For one terrible moment, Jewell thought the sub had been struck by a depth charge. Then he realized it was turbulence that had caused her to tremble so crazily. They had reached the rain squall. He could have cheered out loud. They had done it, they had bloody well done it!

Further up the hull, O'Rourke, not usually the most devout of Catholics, crossed himself and murmured in a dry voice, 'Mother of God, thank ye.' And then, with a sudden revival of his crazy, daredevil Irish spirits, he looked upwards to where the E-boat might well be. 'And bad cess on ye, yer German bugger . . .'

Jewell was no longer listening. Now he had only a matter of minutes to attempt to turn the tables on the German hunter. 'Up periscope,' he commanded. Impatiently he waited for the tube to slide upwards. Twisting his battered cap from front to back, he flung himself behind it, just as the eyepiece broke the surface of the raging sea. Wavelets danced up and down in front of the sight. He caught a glimpse of a lowering sky, black and tormented with jagged arrows of electricity. He even imagined he could hear the ominous drum roll of thunder. With hands that were already wet with sweat once again, he swung the tube round.

There she was. A large German E-boat, a white bone in her teeth, as her sharp prow cleaved the heaving water at speed. The eerie game of lethal hide-and-seek was about to come to an end. In a moment her lookouts would spot the giveaway white foam of the periscope on the surface. But for the moment they had not.

Jewell didn't hesitate. He grabbed the voice tube. Next to him Number One pulled out his stopwatch and tensed. The skipper was going to fire the two 'tin fish'. '*Fire one!*' Jewell commanded.

'*Fire one!*' came back the voice of the torpedo mate.

The *Seraph* shuddered. There was the sharp hush of compressed air. A second later the one ton of sudden death and destruction shot from the rear of the submarine and started tracking to the still unsuspecting E-boat. For a second Jewell watched the wild trail of bubbles which marked its progress before crying, '*Fire two!*'

But there was no need for a second 'tin fish'. A rumble, a blinding flash of violet light, the whole bow of the E-boat rose out of the water as it came to a sudden stop, as if the enemy craft had run into a solid stone wall. For a moment – it seemed an eternity to the awed watcher at the time – the front of the E-boat hung there. An awesome explosion. All around, the watcher through the periscope could see the fragments of wood and steel dropping into the water in a sudden furious rain.

There followed the break-up noises. Even as Jewell knew that he had to lower the periscope and leave the stricken German boat to her fate, he visualized what was happening to her as the bow slapped down once more and internal explosions followed one after another: the bulkheads caving in, the icy sea water rushing in greedily through the great jagged holes in the E-boat's hull, the panic-stricken German sailors fighting and clawing at each other in a desperate attempt to get aloft before it was too late, the young captain bravely trying to keep discipline while his boat sank beneath him.

Then Jewell had seen and heard enough. 'Take her down, Number One,' he ordered. It was as if someone had opened an unseen tap and all energy had drained from his skinny frame. He could do no more.

HMS *Seraph*'s proverbial luck had held once again. But for how much longer, he wondered. Blindly, feeling his way down the narrow corridor between the packed machines, while his crew smiled and muttered, 'Fine work, sir,' and the like, he pulled back the blanket of his little cabin and fell on to his bunk completely exhausted. Within minutes he was snoring, out to the world. Anyone pulling back that blanket then might have thought he was already dead.

Five

There was a knock on the door of Smythe's little room. It was so gentle that he didn't hear it at first. Besides, there was some sort of noisy racket going on outside. Ships' whistles were beginning to shrill urgently and he thought he could hear the sound of cheering further up the docks, where the submarines of the Third Submarine Flotilla were anchored underneath their camouflage netting.

Horatio Smythe stared at himself in the tiny metal shaving mirror. It wasn't so long ago that he had begun shaving in the first place, and although his beard was not particularly strong, he didn't want to nick himself; it didn't look good in an officer who had just been awarded the DSC, the kind of gong that usually older officers won. Besides, he had only one starched clean white collar left and he knew the flag captain was a stickler for a smart turnout; and he still had not lost his Dartmouth fear of being put on report for a sloppy turnout.

The cheering started to become louder. He guessed, as he paused with the safety razor stuck under his soap-covered chin, that some submarine from the Third was coming in after a patrol and was being welcomed back by the men of the Flotilla. He remembered for a moment their own triumphant welcome at Murmansk with the old 'Mucky Duck' at the end of that terrible convoy. For a second he dwelled on how the female Russian skipper of the tug they'd used had taken him down to her cabin and had at last initiated him into the secrets of sexual love.

He sensed a sudden tumescence in his loins at the memory. The thought of her fleshy naked body and the things she had done during that night of wild passion and crazy lust excited him even now. He wet his abruptly dry lips and wondered how he could ever repeat the experience. English women were different, so cool and aloof, save for the women 'Mummy' was always warning him about. He could never imagine them taking his penis into their mouths and doing impossible things to him as she had done, even if a man married them. He shook his head to get what his Mummy always called 'evil thoughts' out of his brain and concentrated on his shaving. He had just sharpened the blade on the inside of a glass like he had seen the ratings do. Still it was blunt and he had to be careful. Then came the knock on the door. It put him off his stroke and he felt a tiny twinge of pain. He had bloody well gone and nicked himself after all!

'Bugger it!' he cursed in the same moment that the door opened slightly and a female voice enquired, 'Lieutenant Smythe, sir?' Even as he dabbed angrily at the blood on his chin, he hoped whoever it was hadn't heard him use such coarse language. His mother had always maintained that a gentleman never swore in the presence of a lady; it simply wasn't the done thing in their circles. That sort of thing was something that low, working-class people did.

'Lieutenant Smythe, sir . . . Can I come through, sir?' It was the pretty young Wren. What was her name? Of course, Wren Tidmus.

'Of course,' he said immediately, brightening up at the sight of her.

She beamed at him. 'Good news, sir. Very good news.' Suddenly her eyes filled with tears, though she caught hold of herself swiftly enough as she added, 'Really good news. The whole of the Third Flotilla is going to celebrate tonight because of it . . .'

Smythe was not really listening. If he had not been such a young man, inhibited by the mores of his class and age, he would have reached out and attempted to comfort her. But he was an Englishman of a type that has long died out: one of those who attempted never to show emotion. It wasn't the done thing. Instead he said, 'Now come on, Wren Tidmus, pull yourself together, young lady. What is this tremendous good news that everyone is going to celebrate this night?'

'Sorry, sir.' She dabbed her eyes. 'I know I'm making a bit

of a fool of myself, sir. But we all admire him so, and when we thought he'd bought it, well . . .'

'Tidmus, *Who . . . what*, please?'

'It's Commander Jewell, sir and his matelots of the *Seraph*. They're safe, sir!' she cried with sudden enthusiasm. 'They're coming in to berth at this very moment. Look out of the window, sir, if you will.'

Razor poised in his hand, a thin trickle of blood coming from his chin, Smythe did as she had commanded.

A small submarine of one of the pre-war classes was ploughing its way down the harbour, her crew, clad in their cleanest white sweaters, lining her battered deck, while on the quays and the other submarines of the Third Flotilla, the ratings and officers cheered and waved their caps. Even the dockyard workers – the hated 'dockies', as the seafaring men called them on account of their thieving habits and their custom of going on strike at the drop of a hat in the middle of total war – were waving.

But it wasn't the *Seraph*'s crew and the cheering spectators that really caught Smythe's attention. It was the black flag bearing the skull and crossbones waving above the conning tower, and the large piece of wreckage just below, adorned with the crooked cross of Nazi Germany. They indicated that the sub which, up to the night before, had been given up as lost on patrol, had not only survived, but had also made a 'kill'. At that moment he realized just why they called Commander Jewell 'a lucky bastard' in the wardroom. He seemed to be one of the few submarine commanders who always returned from a fighting patrol, when most never lasted more than a handful of missions before they were sunk by the enemy.

Wren Tidmus snapped to attention and saluted. 'Sorry to have disturbed you, sir, in your ablutions, but I thought you'd like to know that the *Seraph* had arrived back safely.'

He couldn't return her salute without his cap, but he nodded instead and said, 'Good of you to tell me, Wren Tidmus.'

'One more thing, sir. The flag captain has asked me to inform you that there will be a staff briefing in his office at eight hundred hours tomorrow morning. You and the other SBS officers will attend. Commander Jewell will do the briefing.' She lowered her voice in a conspiratorial manner, as if they were both party to some secret or other. 'But the way those chaps of the Third Flotilla celebrate after a successful patrol, I don't think Commander Jewell will be up to top form.' She saluted again and, doing a smart about turn to reveal shapely legs clad in decidedly unregulation sheer black silk stockings, she marched out.

It was only then, after she had gone, that Smythe realized to his embarrassment that not only had he talked to the pretty Wren with his braces dangling about his hips – something that wouldn't have been approved of at Dartmouth – but he had also forgotten to do up his flies, and the white of his shorts had been on display all the time. 'Oh my sainted aunt!' he moaned, as he made his terrible (for him) discovery. 'What must she think of me?'

In fact, as events would show, Wren Tidmus, she of the sheer black silk stockings, would think very highly indeed of the blushing young officer . . .

As she had predicted, the crew of the *Seraph*, who for security reasons were not allowed to go on the leave which was normally their lot after a wartime patrol, wasted no time in enjoying themselves once they were back on dry land. As he went about his duties, Smythe noted them everywhere, spruced up in their best bell-bottoms, caps tilted in a definitely irregular manner at the backs of their heads, their hair glued well down with brilliantine, 'art-silk' scarves tucked in at their necks, heading for the 'boozers' and the 'knocking shops', as they called the notorious dives of the Hard.

Here and there the dockside police and the shore patrols gave them a hard look, but both the civilian and naval police knew better than to interfere with them now. Half the Third Flotilla would be up in arms if they tried to do so. Besides, who would dare to attempt to stop them enjoying the simple pleasures of the average matelot – 'booze and beaver', as they phrased it – after what they had been through?

Later in the day, Smythe saw them come staggering back, happy but broke, most of them – and in some cases being actually carried in by cursing, sweating, burly naval policemen, singing their drunken heads off about '*the mate at the wheel had a ruddy good feel at the girl I left behind me*' and other such sentimental ditties.

Once, as the officers settled down in the wardroom after dinner to enjoy ITMA and Tommy Handley, their evening relaxation was disturbed by an old three-striper from the *Seraph* who decided to serenade the amused officers with his own rendition of 'Colonel Bogey' – '*Where was the engine driver when the boiler bust? They found his bollocks, and the same to you. Boll*—' until a brawny petty officer from the officers' kitchen grabbed him and threatened him with the 'rattle', if he 'didn't frigging well belt up here and frigging now'. With the petty officer's arm round his neck, half-choking him, the three-striper had no other alternative. Thus he departed and an amused silence descended upon the wardroom until the flag captain cleared the air with, 'Well, you can't blame him, chaps, after what he and those other brave fellers have just been through, can you?' That was the signal to turn up ITMA once again and be treated to Mrs Mop entering with her famous catchphrase, 'Can I do you now, sir?'

By midnight the barracks that housed the sailors from the Third were quiet once more, save for some poor soul, moaning drunkenly in the 'heads' that 'My guts is falling out. Holy Mary, Mother o' God, why did I drink that sodding rotgut?' Which would be followed by the start of another series of painful groans and desperate farts.

Listening with his window open, for it was a hot June night, Smythe wondered how he was going to deal with a bunch of tough matelots like the crew of the *Seraph* obviously were, when it came to his turn to be one of the veteran submarine's officers. Despite his gong, he felt inadequate when faced with such a brave and bold bunch as they were. Besides, what did he really know about subs? Indeed, he had only the most rudimentary knowledge of how submarines worked. How could he face matelots, volunteers all, who had probably been in subs ever since they had passed out from recruit training?

As the bugler over at the Royal Marines quarters opposite sounded 'lights out', young Smythe finally drifted off to a troubled sleep, the moaning of O'Rourke in the heads receding into the far reaches of his mind. But it wasn't the uncertain future that made the young man toss from side to side in his rumpled bed, it was the dream: the kind that had always plagued the dreams of young men in their sexual prime.

At first he couldn't quite grasp who the naked young woman was, cavorting lecherously in front of him, displaying all her physical charms in a manner that had him panting hard in his sleep, his loins moving back and forth instinctively as if he was already copulating with her. His only experience so far had been with the Russian woman in Murmansk, and he gasped, '*Davai*,' his only word of Russian, which she had taught him in the middle of that sweat-soaked, wildly thrilling night in the tightness of her bunk. 'Come . . . come . . . !'

But the naked woman, her breasts like melons swinging to left and right every time she moved in that maddeningly provocative dance, holding out her hands almost pleadingly for him to embrace her, didn't react. Then he saw that she was not totally naked after all. Below that delightful 'V' of pubic hair, she was wearing sheer black stockings!

In his dream he gasped. The naked siren, dancing and enticing him to God knows what obscene sexual practices, her legs spread now so that he could see the wet pink slit which was the source of all depraved sexual pleasure, was no other than Wren Titmus. As he gawped, open mouthed and gasping, his body working in and out as if he were in that final frenetic race for carnal culmination, he felt he was about to burst. In a moment he knew even in his dream he would explode, her writhing, sinuous sweat-lathered body tormenting him beyond all measure.

Abruptly, with a great start, before that final tremor swept through him which he could not have stopped, he awoke. The throbbing erection disappeared as swiftly as it had come as he realized with a terrible sense of shame what had nearly happened to him – what *he* had almost let happen. It was something that the older boys at his prep school had giggled and tittered about. 'Did you hear the tale of the chap who went to sleep with a problem on his mind and awoke with the solution in his hand?' *A wet dream!* A sordid business which had

45

disgusted him even then. After all, a chap was supposed to be able to control himself at all times.

Parched and ashamed of himself, checking the front of his pyjama trousers, he padded on his bare feet to the little wash-basin. Hastily he washed his flushed, sweaty face and then had a drink of cool water from his tooth glass.

A noise caught his attention. Under other circumstances he would have ignored it; like most young men he needed a lot of sleep. But at this particular moment he didn't feel like going to bed immediately. He didn't want a repetition of that wild sexual dream, which had degraded Wren Tidmus into a bawdy object of his base desires. So he padded over to the un-blacked-out window and peered out in an attempt to discover the source of the noise.

Below, the square was in darkness save for a patch of hard silver light cast by the sickle moon, busy skidding from cloud to cloud, and for a moment he couldn't see anything. He frowned and was about to return to his bed when he spotted the red glow of a cigarette or pipe. A second later a figure hunched in a shabby woollen bathrobe came into view, battered white officer's cap on his head, puffing hard at a briar pipe, obviously trying hard to keep the dottle burning.

Smythe's frown deepened. What was an officer doing out there at this time of night, clad in a bathrobe and carpet slippers; and a senior officer to boot, to judge from the gold braid which adorned his battered white cap?

Suddenly the lone figure paused and looked up, as if he suspected he was watched. Hastily Smythe dodged behind the blackout curtain. But even as he did so he recognized the officer standing there, puffing at his pipe in the middle of the night. He had seen him in the group photograph of the *Seraph*'s officers and petty officers which adorned the ward-room wall not far from that of the King-Emperor. It was Lt Commander Jewell, the hero of the recent patrol. Then the officer passed slowly out of sight, leaving Smythe alone with his bewilderment, sex forgotten now. When everyone else of his crew had been out celebrating and were presumably drunk and out to the world in their bunks now, why was the commander walking the square, and obviously stone-cold sober, at this time of the night? It was a question that the young officer would puzzle over for the rest of that night, but one for which he had no answer . . .

Six

'*Swing them arms!*' the ancient petty officer screeched at the top of his voice. 'Bags o' swank now – remember who you are. Left, right . . . Left, right.' Panting, red-faced and sweating, the new recruits flung up their arms as if the limbs were going to fly from their sockets at any moment. 'Come on, you bunch o' pregnant penguins, get them legs open. If anything falls out, yer friendly old PO'll pick 'em up for yer . . . Left, right . . . left, right.'

Smythe grinned and remembered how it had been at Dartmouth: the same hectic, flustered recruits and the same old wizened petty officers. As he fumbled for his pass, he told himself there had to be a special school for breeding old petty officers, with their gimlet eyes.

The marine sentry, armed with rifle and fixed bayonet, took his time examining Smythe's pass, and the latter guessed that this was going to be no ordinary routine briefing; the sentry was too fussy. Finally the marine was satisfied. He handed the pass back, shouting, 'Thank you, sir!' at the top of his voice, and stamped his gleaming boot down, as if he were trying to break through the concrete below.

Symthe passed through into the inner room, where two or three officers in camouflage smocks with the insignia of the Special Boat Service lounged in the beaten-up horsehair chairs, smoking fitfully under the watchful gaze of a middle-aged officer wearing the medal ribbons of the old war, who had Naval Intelligence written all over him.

'Smythe,' he announced himself. The big burly commandos nodded idly, as the man from Naval Intelligence came over and whispered as if he wished even his name to be kept secret, 'Wilkinson, Naval Intelligence.' They shook hands.

Wilkinson's hand was dry as bone; Smythe might well have been clutching the hand of someone long dead. 'Remember, young Smythe. What you'll hear is most secret. Remember, too, you are bound by the Official Secrets Act. Blab anything you're told here to a third party and . . .'

'And they'll be stringing you up from the yardarm of the *Victory* over there,' the nearest SBS officer, a big fellow with a tremendous billowing moustache cut in cheerfully. 'Sambo Simpson.' He reached out a big hard hand. 'Late of the Kenya Light Infantry. Hence the nickname – Sambo. The white man's burden, you know.' He gave that booming laugh of his once more.

Smythe smiled. For Pongoes they didn't seem bad chaps.

Wilkinson opened his mouth to say something. But was beaten to it by the locked door being opened by the marine sentry to allow in the same lieutenant commander whom Smythe had seen the night before wandering around the parade ground in his shabby bathrobe. But this morning Commander Jewell was smart and erect in his best tunic, medal ribbons adorning his chest, his blue eyes quick and alert, taking in the whole room in a flash, until his gaze came to rest on Smythe.

Obviously he knew Wilkinson and the SBS officers, for he gave them a quick, 'Good morning, gentlemen. Glad to see you aboard once more,' before turning to Smythe. 'Ah, our young hero, eh.' He indicated the ribbon of the DSC on the younger officer's chest. 'Good show. Got yourself wounded again, what!' He nodded at the bloody scratch on Smythe's chin where he had cut himself yet again. Hastily Smythe tucked in his neck so that the commander couldn't see his blood-stained shirt.

Jewell reached out his hand and shook Smythe's firmly, saying, 'Good to have you aboard, too, Smythe.' His smile vanished. 'All right, let's get down to business. We've not a lot of time. Wilkinson –' he turned to the middle-aged Intelligence officer – 'give 'em the classy chat about the cosmos, pray.'

Wilkinson frowned, but it was obvious he was used to the breezy, disrespectful manner of these young submarine commanders, fated to die violently sooner or later. For he launched into his part of the briefing almost immediately, while the SBS officers fiddled with their pipes and appeared to be paying very little attention to what he had to say.

'I won't bore you with the details, gentlemen,' Wilkinson said.

'That'll be the day,' the SBS officer known as Sambo commented. Obviously he had been briefed by Wilkinson before.

'But I'll just say that we are not on the best of terms with the French. That is, the Vichy French, who you might know are working actively with the German occupiers both in continental France and the French colonies abroad, especially those in French North Africa.'

It was then that Smythe remembered the tropical kit he had been ordered to draw from the stores a couple of days before. Did that mean the operation which was being discussed here was connected with the French North African colonies?

Wilkinson enlightened him the next moment. He walked across to the back of the briefing room, where the map board was covered by a black cloth and a notice stating, *To All Officers – this curtain must not be moved without permission.*

Slowly, even dramatically for such a dry-as-dust person, Wilkinson started to pull the little rope. Outside, the ancient petty officer drilling the recruits was barking, 'Now get this, you dozy lot, on the command "one", you raise yer left foot – that's the one opposite yer right one, got it? At the same time, you raise yer right arm parallel to yer shoulder. On the command "two" . . .'

Smythe forgot the ancient drill NCO, as the map was fully revealed. There were displayed France's North African possessions, with a series of red chinagraph marks on the coast of her largest colony, Algeria. He frowned thoughtfully. From the 'buzzes' he had picked up in the wardroom ever since he had arrived in Pompey, he had thought that the clandestine operations carried out by Commander Jewell's *Seraph* had been close-range ones, probably mainland France on the whole. Now it seemed as if a very long-range op indeed was being proposed. All the same, he was still very puzzled. What role would he play in such an op? After all, he had no real training in submarines.

Wilkinson rambled on, sketching in the difficult and complicated political situation in North Africa, in particular in Algeria. There the German Control Commission were the real bosses, although the French, who supported the pro-German French government in Vichy, ran the colony still. There were, however, a few French there who supported the exiled French Government in London under General de Gaulle, but not many. One thing was certain, as Wilkinson said in that dogmatic fashion of his. 'All of them – Germans, Vichy French and de Gaulle French, the whole lot of them – dislike us intensely.'

Sambo Simpson grunted. 'That's nothing new, Wilkers, old bean. Everybody knows that the Froggies are jealous of us. God knows why we ever took up with them. I 'spect it all started at Trafalgar when old Nelson knocked seven bells out of their navy. Besides, what can you make of a nation that makes love with its ruddy tongue?' Again he gave that great booming laugh of his, which in time Smythe would come to dread.

Wilkinson faltered to a stop and Jewell said, 'All right, Sambo, that's enough of that,' adding, 'I'll take over now, Wilkinson.'

Gratefully Wilkinson nodded his agreement. He had obviously had enough of 'Sambo'.

'Well, chaps, this is the drill,' Jewell commenced in his businesslike manner. 'Our orders are to land a party on the coast of Algeria. Here, at a small bay near the village of Cherchell. Strange name for an Arabic place, isn't it? Reminds me of the PM's residence at Chartwell. No matter. It's about seventy-five miles west of the Algerian capital of Algiers. According to Lieutenant Wilkinson here, it is on a coast that is especially well guarded.'

'Yessir. Not only do the Vichy French guard it, but the Hun does too. The French are after smugglers from the French mainland. The Germans are looking for enemy saboteurs and spies and the like,' Wilkinson volunteered hastily.

'Bloody Frog saboteurs,' another of the SBS officers snorted in a thick Ulster accent. 'Allus stink of cheap scent like that stuff shop girls buy at Woolworths.'

51

Jewell allowed himself a grin at the Ulsterman's comment. The former Ulster Rifleman was as straight-laced and moral as they came, in the grim protestant tradition of the province, but he was one hell of a fighter when the chips were down. 'Brave men all the same, Ferguson.'

'I suppose so, sir. But this isn't going to be one of the *Seraph*'s most exciting assignments, is it?'

'I don't know. It will be if the Germans catch you. They're the ones, so Wilkinson tells me, you have to fear in Algeria, though the French haven't been treating any of our people who have fallen into their hands with kid gloves.'

'Thank you, sir, for the encouraging words.'

Smythe smiled. He liked the SBS men's banter. They were obviously a tough, experienced bunch. Still, he wondered what role he was going to take in this strange long-range enterprise to North Africa.

Jewell soon enlightened him. He turned to Smythe, smiling a little as he did so. 'Now, my young hero,' he said. 'I suppose you're wondering what all this has got to do with you?' He didn't wait for the younger officer to reply, but went on with: 'Navigation off the spot where we've decided to land these people is tricky. It's easily missed, located as it is between two hill features. There are tricky rip tides too, which could easily put the moppers on accurate navigation and endanger the whole op. So this is where you come in, Smythe.'

'Sir?'

'These gentleman of the SBS, as experienced as they are in clandestine ops, are still not the best of sailors. Besides, we've never landed "Joes"* from so far out before. So I need a trained navigator. You've done the Dartmouth course and you've handled a badly damaged craft, that *Black Swan* of yours, in the tricky waters of the North Atlantic.'

Smythe felt he was going to blush again as usual and prayed he wouldn't in front of these hardboiled older officers.

'Anyway,' Jewell was saying, 'their Lordships think you're the best man for the job. Otherwise you wouldn't be here,

*'Joes', slang name used by Intelligence for the spies, saboteurs etc they were running into German-occupied territory.

52

Smythe. So you've got it. While the gentlemen from the SBS are concentrating on getting their people ashore, you'll be guiding them in. Clear?'

'Clear, sir,' Smythe heard himself saying, with more confidence than he felt.

'Now then,' Jewell continued, face hard now, his smile vanished. 'Let's get down to details. We sail in forty-eight hours' time. So, from fifteen hundred hours this afternoon, all personnel involved will be confined to barracks. That means you gentlemen too, and Wilkinson here as well.'

Sambo Simpson groaned. 'Have a heart, Commander. I've got a hot date with an even hotter blonde – and I'll be finding out she isn't a true blonde, if you follow my meaning?'

Ferguson, the Ulster puritan, frowned and Jewell snapped, 'Come on, Sambo! No time for that now.'

'Sorry sir.'

'We sail on the evening tide then, in two days' time. Our destination is Gibraltar, where we pick up, er –' for some reason, Jewell hesitated momentarily – 'our Joes.'

Ferguson noted the hesitation. He said, 'Seems an important op, this one, sir. I mean, there are subs at Malta that could carry out a Joe landing just as well as we can. Besides, sir, there are umpteen smugglers – which I know from personal experience when our squadron was based in Alex – working from little ports all over the Med, who could do the same job for coin of the realm.' He made the Continental gesture of counting money with his finger and thumb. 'What's so important about this mission that we have to sail all the way from Pompey to Gib in order to carry it out, sir?'

Jewell hesitated. Outside, the petty officer drill instructor was shouting, *'Now then, I'm gonna show you bunch o' frigging heroes how to get on parade proper-like. Pin back yer lugs and let yer frigging shell-likes take this in . . . Cos I'm only gonna say it once . . . On the command . . . Right markers – you tall streaks o' piss I've just picked will march smartly on to the square, all bull and bags o' swank . . .'*

Jewell opened his mouth, and in years to come the future Vice-Admiral Horatio Smythe, DSO, DSC would always remember that moment when his life changed – the old petty officer yelling his head off, the SBS officers lounging in the battered horsehair chairs, Wilkinson looking apprehensive, as if he were afraid that Jewell was going to say too much, and Commander Jewell, the sub ace, abruptly looking much older than his actual age, and apprehensive, as if he had just realized the full importance of what he was about to say. 'This, gentlemen, is top secret,* as we have to call it.' He licked his lips, which were suddenly very dry. 'It definitely mustn't go any further than this room. Indeed, I'm risking a court martial by revealing our cargo to you now. But I believe you ought to know what you're letting yourselves in for.' He flashed a glance at the guarded door, as if he half suspected someone might be listening there, before saying in a hushed whisper, 'The *Seraph* is to land a full American general and his staff in North Africa. Why –' he shrugged – 'I don't know.'

'Christ Almighty!' Sambo Simpson gasped. '*A Yank general!*' But that was the only reaction to Commander Jewell's revelation. The rest remained frozen there in silence, as if in the final scene of some cheap melodrama.

*Before the Americans entered the war, the usage was 'most secret'.

Seven

The two American generals in their best Class A uniform waited till the English women drivers had drawn away from in front of Number 10 Downing Street before the smaller of the two whispered, 'Remember, Wayne, the guy's a lush. They say the President called him "a drunken bum" and I've heard from brother Milton in Washington that Hoover of the FBI has done an investigation on his drinking habits for FDR.'

The taller of the two new generals sniffed and said, also sotto voce, just in case anyone opened the door, which was protected by sandbags, and heard what they were whispering about, 'What a dandy set-up, Ike! A US president who's a cripple* and an English prime minister who's addicted to the bottle. How in Sam Hill's name are we gonna win the war with two guys like that in charge, eh?'

The smaller general gave that ear-to-ear grin which would soon be famous throughout the free world and said, 'Well, Wayne, be that as it may, our job is to win the war despite one being a cripple and the other being a drunk. 'Kay, let's make our mark, have a drink and get the hell out of here. I've got one hell of a day in front of me tomorrow.'

Thus the two old friends, who had been together ever since they had entered military service nearly thirty years before, Generals Eisenhower and Wayne Clark, his deputy, straightened their shoulders, bracing themselves as if they were young cadets back at West Point, responded to the salute of the two rigid Grenadier Guardsmen guarding the door and knocked on the residence of Winston Spencer Churchill. After nearly two

*US President Franklin Delano Roosevelt had been crippled by polio since 1921.

55

years of plotting and wheedling, Churchill's 'special relationship' with the United States (as he fancied it was) was at last to take on a tangible form.

The door was opened at once, as if someone behind it had been waiting all along for the two American 'new boys' to make their appearance. An ancient servant in rusty black croaked, 'Come right in, gentlemen. The blackout, you know. The Prime Minister is waiting for you.'

Hurriedly as if they feared the chink of yellow light slicing the inky darkness outside might reveal the position of Number Ten to some German bomber lurking overhead, the two Americans squeezed by the ancient servant into the hall of the PM's residence, to be met by a hearty, somewhat slurred voice coming from the stairs.

'Welcome gentlemen . . . welcome indeed to my home!'

It was the great man himself, wearing scuffed carpet slippers and a kind of dirty painter's smock, and, for some reason, minus his false teeth. Churchill waved his big cigar at the somewhat bewildered Americans, saying, 'Not much to compare with your own White House. But still, unlike we naughty British, the Hun has not yet been able to burn down Number Ten.'

For a moment, the two Americans were puzzled by the remark, until the taller of the two grinned and said, 'You mean when you Britishers burnt it down in the War of 1812, sir?'

Churchill nodded and gave them an impish grin, while the smaller of the two Americans said, 'Well, sir, it looks as if the Hun hasn't given up trying yet.' He jerked his head to the east, where the air-raid sirens were beginning to wail once again.

Churchill didn't lose his grin. 'Oh that, we'll soon see them off, General – er . . .'

'Eisenhower, sir.'

'General Eisenhower. Yes, we've seen them off before, we'll do it again, never fear, especially now that you, our cousins from over the sea, have come to join us.' Churchill crossed to the wall of the entrace hall and rubbed his back up and down against it like a dog with fleas. 'Now then,' he said, as he ceased the movement that made his toothless jowls wobble energetically, 'let's have a drink and discuss this damned French situation. But I'll tell you this, General – er – Eisenhower, if I could meet Admiral Darlan, much as I hate him, I would cheerfully crawl on my hands and knees for a mile if by doing so I could get him to bring the French fleet of his over to us.' So saying, the PM waved his big cigar at them to follow him into the library, where already a large silver tray of all sorts of hard liquour had been set out for his visitors – and naturally himself – as if they had a long drinking session before them.

Eisenhower gave his old friend Wayne Clark a look which said, 'I told you so, didn't I? He's a lush, isn't he?' All the same, he accepted what the PM called a 'cocktail' from the Prime Minister though for life of him he could not identify what kind it was, save that it contained some very strong waters indeed. In fact, his first sip kept him coughing for at least a minute.

Churchill didn't seem to notice. Smoking and drinking at the same time, he launched immediately into the business of the evening. 'I want troops pouring into French North Africa. I want them coming through the walls, the ceilings, everywhere. The French will go with us, if they see us winning. But they can't afford to pick a loser. That's where you gentlemen from America come in. The French believe you contributed a major part to their success in World War One, when they were down after their defeats of 1917. Now if they see a larger US presence in North Africa, even if we supply most of the troops and dress them up in American uniforms –' he winked roguishly – 'then their generals and admirals will come over to us.'

Time passed. Churchill rang a bell. A valet appeared, as if by magic. Churchill never ceased talking while the Americans watched in amazement as he held up his feet and the valet started to change his socks. A light meal followed. Churchill ate with an appetite. Bent low over the bowl, so that his nose was almost in the liquid, he spooned up the soup till it was all gone, whereupon he bawled and rattled the bowl with his spoon like a spoiled child in the nursery. *'More soup, I say . . .*

more soup!' And all the while he and they drank – 'cocktails', red wine, brandy and soda, anything and everything alcoholic.

The initial hesitation of the two American generals vanished. Clark, red-faced and eyes gleaming, waved his arms around excitedly as he told Churchill they should have American paratroopers landing in French North Africa with parachutes made of Stars and Stripes banners. There should be skywriters buzzing back and forth over the African sky inscribing the words for all to see and remind the French of their debt to America: *'Vive la France, Lafayette . . . We are here agin – for the second time!'*

It was all great fun, and the two Americans, now quite drunk, didn't realize that the host had long begun to taper off his drinking, though he remained as exuberant and enthusiastic as he had been at the beginning of their meeting. Slowly the PM started to bring the conversation round to the mission for Clark, which he had previously proposed to Roosevelt and which the President had then ordered Eisenhower to have his old friend Clark carry out.

With an air of finality, he downed his brandy and soda and said to Clark, whom Churchill was now calling, on account of the General's large beaky nose 'My American Eagle', 'General Eisenhower here and I have a mission for you, American Eagle . . . A dangerous one!'

Clark, whose sole experience of combat had been thirty minutes in the frontline in 1918, when he had been wounded clambering into the trenches in France, stopped drinking abruptly, glass poised in mid-air. 'Dangerous?' he queried.

Churchill laughed. The veteran of three wars, who had never feared danger and sudden death in battle, was always surprised when men seemed to be afraid of dying in combat. 'Never fear, my brave American Eagle. It is dangerous, but vitally important to the Allied cause. And I can assure you that during this mission you will be protected by the best men the British Royal Navy can provide.'

Eisenhower nodded his head encouragingly.

'You see, "Torch" – the codename for our invasion of French North Africa, as you know – offers the greatest opportunity that England has experienced in these many years. President

Roosevelt feels the same. Both FDR and I are prepared to help in any way we can. But the important thing is this. The first battle we must win is the *battle to have no battle with the French.*'

Alarmed at the thought of danger, Clark was still drunk enough not to understand what the PM was getting at. Eisenhower, who was slightly less drunk, enlightened him. 'You see, Wayne, the French have a hundred and fifty thousand regular troops in North Africa, plus two hundred thousand reservists – that's more than we and the British can field to invade the place. So if we can we must convince the French they shouldn't oppose our landings there. If they did . . .' He shrugged eloquently and let an eager Churchill take over again.

'We already know from events in Syria and other parts of Africa that the French will fight us if we invade their territory, especially when their officers loyal to Vichy have their say, which they mostly do in North Africa at the moment. Fortunately however, we have discovered there is one senior French officer over there who might come over to our side – he hates the Hun and the fact that the French are having to take orders from the German enemy. He is General Charles Emmanuel Mast, deputy commander of the nineteenth French Infantry Corps, ideally stationed in the Algiers area, the seat of the French administration.' Churchill paused dramatically, raising one finger as if he were addressing the packed House of Commons. 'Mast, my dear American Eagle, is the man you are going to see to convince him to throw in his lot with us and stop any French defence of the Algerian coastline.'

As drunk as he was, General Clark whistled with surprise at the magnitude of the task that Churchill had sprung on him so suddenly and so surprisingly. He flashed Eisenhower a glance, but the latter looked away as if he were abruptly embarrassed. Suddenly Clark remembered that, earlier on, the PM had mentioned his assignment might be dangerous. Hastily he asked, 'But where am I going to meet this – er – General Mast, sir?'

Churchill hesitated for a second, as if he were reluctant to speak and reveal the secret rendezvous.

In the meantime, Eisenhower jumped in and said, 'As the

59

Prime Minister has said, Wayne, you will be well taken care of and protected by his best men.'

Clark wasn't appeased. Angrily he demanded, '*Where?*'

Churchill gave him a toothless smile, but his gaze remained wary, as if he were now wondering if his 'American Eagle' were up to the task before him. By now he knew something about Clark from his own people in Washington. There, the lean six-foot-three-inch lieutenant-general, who had been a mere major two years before, was not well liked. He was regarded as too ambitious and a relentless promoter of himself in military and political circles. One of his rivals, an elderly gentleman called Patton, had told the British military attaché in the American capital that 'He seems to me to be more preoccupied with bettering his own future than winning the war.' Now the PM, a shrewd manipulator of other men's weaknesses when he had to, said, 'But my dear American Eagle, if you can bring Mast over to our side, we will probably be able to gain entry into French North Africa without a shot being fired.' He beamed at a suddenly mollified Clark. 'Imagine the glory of it. You'll go down in history, my dear fellow. The man who conquered North Africa with hardly a shot being fired. Even my General Montgomery, as boastful as he is, couldn't claim that out there in the Western Desert.'

Clark's mood changed almost immediately. 'Do you think so, sir?'

'Yes, I certainly do . . . So, where do you meet Mast?' Churchill answered his own question. 'In North Africa, not far from the capital, Algiers.' He lowered his voice, as if he expected trouble. 'How do you get there?' Again he answered his own question. 'I'm afraid you're not going to like it much, due to your great height . . . *By submarine!*'

Even that didn't dampen Clark's new enthusiasm for this historic mission. Wasn't he going to pull off the greatest American diplomatic coup of the new war? He'd go down in the history books. 'That doesn't worry me, sir,' he chortled and raised his glass. 'Here's to the success of the Clark-Mast meeting, sir.'

Dutifully, Eisenhower, sober too by now, raised his own

glass, as well. 'Here's to the success of the Clark-Mast meeting!'

Watching the two, the tall craggy general with his great beak of a nose, face flushed with both wine and enthusiasm, and the pudgy-faced old man without teeth, Eisenhower, who was nobody's fool, told himself that, for a 'drunken bum', the Englishman was a very sharp operator, a very sharp one indeed. Very cleverly he had passed the buck to the new American ally. If they screwed it up, it would be no fault of the British. He sighed and told himself Churchill was going to be someone he would have to watch carefully.

Book Two

Trapped!

'I know of no case where a man added to his dignity
by standing on it.'

Winston Churchill

One

HMS *Seraph* sailed on the evening tide. Silently, secretively. Now there was none of the wild cheering and hooting of ships' whistles which had greeted her return from her last mission in the France. The authorities had waited till the dockers and port workers had left the port after the end of the day shift. In addition they had postponed the night shift for several hours till the submarine had cleared Portsmouth. As for the sailors of the Third Submarine Flotilla, they had been confined to barracks till reveille on the following morning. Thus it was clear to everyone on board the departing submarine that her mission was so vital that the authorities were risking shutting down Britain's key naval port for nearly half a day in order to preserve the secrecy of HMS *Seraph*'s departure.

Smythe, together with the other SBS officers who had been allowed on the conning tower by Commander Jewell to get a 'last breath of decent air' before the submarine submerged once she reached the open sea, realized that now they were coming to the end of the summer. Night was falling earlier than ever. Great shadows were sweeping across the land, obscuring whatever lights were still allowed to burn, and that smell of summer – drying hay, the sweetness of newly mown grass – had vanished. The land smelled of approaching winter and the fresh hardships that wartime winters always brought with them.

At other times the young officer would have been a little downcast at that knowledge, and the fact that he was sailing into the unknown, perhaps never to return. Now, however, his young mind was too full of yesterday and what Wren Tidmus – *no*, he must learn to call her Gloria – had done for him in her shy embarrassed way. He knew that she had not wanted to do it – what pleasure had she received from the act, he asked himself. None, he guessed. But she *had* wanted to please him. What had she whispered shyly, as her delicate little hand had groped hesitantly inside his flies? 'I just want to give you something to remember me by, Horatio,' she had breathed. 'Just in case . . .' She had broken off there and he knew why. She had thought he might not be coming back, as so many young men who went to sea in submarines didn't.

'Penny for them, young hero?' It was Sambo Simpson, who had clattered aloft with a huge commando dagger in his big hand and now commenced sharpening it on a whetstone. 'Are you getting soppy about leaving that lovely piece of Wren crackling behind, what?' He grinned lecherously.

The big SBS man didn't mean his comment maliciously, but Smythe flushed and said hotly, 'She's not like that, Sambo.'

'All women are, young feller-me-lad,' Simpson replied, not put out in any way. 'Especially if you've got them on their backs and in the right frame of mind, if you follow my meaning. Go at it like bloody fiddlers' elbows, even yer simpering English roses in their twinsets and cardigans. Mark my words, young hero, the colonel's lady and Rosie O'Grady, as someone once said, are both the same with their knickers off.'

Perhaps in years to come, the future Vice-Admiral Horatio Smythe, steeped by then in ancient lecheries, might think like that, but not then. His jaw hardened, his eyes blazed and, with his fists clenched, he was about to launch into – at least – a verbal attack on the big captain, when Commander Jewell said quietly, 'I think, gentlemen, we've seen the last of England for this day. Pray go below. I'm going to dive soon . . .'

Three and a half thousand miles away at another Pompey and across the river at the great US staging area of Hampton Roads, thousands upon thousands of American sailors and soldiers were also preparing to make the long voyage into the unknown, which would finally take them to French North Africa. They were part of the three convoys which would carry nearly a quarter of a million American and British troops to invade the three French colonies.

On the surface, the preparations for the long voyage seemed

chaotic. For everything had to be included in the troopships and freighters that would take the troops and their supplies to countries that most of the invading GIs had never even heard of. And, as was customary in that great country, most of its ordinary citizens had only the vaguest idea of the geography of anywhere outside their own continent.

Everything from cranberry sauce for the troops' Thanksgiving Dinner to contraceptives – 'What we gonna do – fuck them into submission?' – had to be included in the massive build-up for what was to come.

French dictionaries had to be purchased in bulk. Cooks were taught how to prepare rice dishes just in case the first prisoners ate rice instead of 'good ole American taters'. Half a million dollars worth of tea had been purchased to entertain the tea-swallowing limeys, who might have to live with their American allies – God forbid! That summer a nationwide Gallup poll indicated that 60 per cent of the US population didn't trust the British. Churchill and Roosevelt were routinely booed by movie audiences whenever they appeared in the newsreels. Five million dollars in gold had been hurriedly acquired, mostly from Canada, to bribe the natives, because everyone knew that the 'towelheads', as they would soon be called, always had their palms greased before they did anything. They were as goddam lazy as the Southern negro.

Not that the GIs believed for one instant they were going anywhere where there would be natives. The issue of tropical kit and booklets on how not to spit in front of the local mosque – those towelheads didn't like it – and the daily learning chant in French, '*Nous sommes les américains . . . nous sommes vos amis,*' were all part of a great deception. In reality, the great convoy would sail first southwards to avoid the German U-boats in the North Atlantic, and then, when it was off the Azores, would swing north and then head for 'Old Jolly', as Bob Hope, the comedian, was now calling it. Once in England, the GIs quipped, they'd be employed 'wiping the bird shit off the White Cliffs of Dover for the rest of the war'.*

*A pun on the popular song of the time with its sentimental text about the bluebirds over the white cliffs of Dover.

67

Not that the young draftees, away from home for the first time, cared where they were going to at that moment. Apart from food, their primary interest was sex. They scorned the 'entertainment' offered by their regimental bands, who marched up and down playing the old high-school marches, always ending with 'The Star Spangled Banner' followed by the British anthem, 'God Save the King', and the 'Marseillaise' in rotating order.

But it wasn't Sousa and his rousing fast marches that set the young men's blood tingling; it was the thought of the cheap whores who had thronged to the staging area in their thousands by the time the ships were ready to sail. It was no use issuing booklets warning, *One of the deep-down urges that must be controlled is sex*. If they were going to die, the young men told themselves, they were going to get laid first. They weren't going to die without losing their cherry, no sirree!

In Britain, where another great convoy of American and British troops would set sail for the first great allied attack of the war, things were even worse. The quartermasters had already 'lost' some 260,000 tons of supplies which had been sent from the States for the assault, and Eisenhower was forced to cable Washington asking whether the War Department would consider sending another duplicate shipment, which would keep the invaders in food and ammunition for a month and a half. The War Department would – and that was 'misplaced' too. Indeed, 20 per cent of all the supplies intended for the Anglo-American invasion of French North Africa was pilfered by the notoriously light-fingered British 'dockies'. Even when supplies arrived safely they were unloaded haphazardly and thus lost. One US Army regiment had its men and equipment delivered to Britain in fifty-five different ships. If that wasn't bad enough, the crates with the men's equipment, including the ammunition they'd need for the weapons during the initial landing, was buried among the hundreds of crates lining the docks and was never found again. That day Eisenhower had to 'borrow' one million rounds of rifle ammunition from the British. But the 'snafu'*, as the GIs called it

*Situation normal, all fucked up.

crudely, didn't seem to worry the future 'Supreme Commander'. Two days later he sent another urgent cable to Washington for a 'bullet-proof, seven-passenger automobile of normal appearance'. Already the soldier, who had been a lowly colonel two years before, looking forward to a slippered retirement in a warmer part of the States, where he could eke out his miserable pension, was beginning to acquire the airs and graces of a major military-political leader.

Young Horatio Smythe, buried in the fetid cramped interior of HMS *Seraph*, where one sea-water toilet had to serve the needs of over forty men, naturally knew nothing of all this – the great armada that would sail after them if the unknown American general they were to carry to North Africa completed his mission successfully.

He, like those young American soldiers far off in Virginia, was concerned, too, with his own personal life. Often when he could lie in a bunk, still hot from the body of some petty officer who had just gone on watch, he indulged himself in day-dreaming about that last day with Wren Tidmus and what she had done for him. It had been a warm afternoon that day of Commander Jewell's final briefing when he had bumped into her.

Perhaps on account of the warmth, she had shed her usual navy-blue tunic for the Wrens' simple white cotton blouse that reached prudishly right up to her neck. But the warmth had made it stick to her upper body tightly, so that her splendid breasts were displayed to perfection.

He had swallowed hard at the sight, especially as her nipples, pert and erect, pressed hard at the thin white material so that he imagined that he could actually see them through her blouse and bra.

As usual she had saluted. But neither she nor he had taken the difference in their ranks too seriously this time – perhaps she, too, knew of his immediate departure. In fact, Wren Tidmus gave a look that Mummy might well have called that of a 'sly minx'. But then, Mummy was always worried that he might fall for a women who wouldn't be worthy of the name of Smythe. She was desperately keen that in 'these times

69

when women have no shame or morals' he shouldn't allow himself to be trapped into a wartime marriage by some 'lower-class hussy' pretending that she had been made pregnant by him.

Not that the manner in which Wren Tidmus had made love to him that late afternoon could ever have resulted in her becoming pregnant. As she had whispered to him while they lay in the long grass below Southsea, her head hung modestly, 'I've never done . . . *it.*'

He had kissed her passionately. 'I don't want you to, if you don't want to.' Though at that moment, with his erection thrusting urgently through the cloth of his trousers, he was begging inwardly for relief from the strain of unrequited sexual lust; he had even forgotten his mother's warnings and his own fear of what might happen if he did get a girl pregnant.

'But I know from the other Wrens that a girl can help a man when he's . . .' She had left the rest of the sentence unfinished, as if she were too embarrassed to continue.

'Aroused?'

She had nodded numbly, her head still hanging so that he could not see her eyes.

He had licked suddenly parched lips and after a while had dared to ask in a voice he hardly recognized as his own, 'How?'

It seemed to take her an age to reply. 'Like this,' she answered in a little girl's voice, and her hand had wandered to his loins, touching that bulge so that he felt for an instant he might finish there and then. And she had begun undoing his flies.

Without another word, her delicate fingers had wandered, found the opening in his underpants and seized his penis delicately, so delicately that he thought he might well black out with the utter, unbelievable delight of it all.

He hadn't. Her hand had moved swiftly. Up and down. He felt he had never experienced such sublime ectasy, even with the Russian woman in Murmansk. Up and down. Faster and faster. He groaned with pleasure. 'More!' he gasped. 'Please, more, darling . . . *You must!*' he cried through gritted teeth, his voice hard, cruel, commanding. '*More!*' He had pressed her hand with his, making sure she wouldn't stop now. 'Yes . . .

70

yes,' she gasped, as if she, too, were enjoying the impossible thrill of it all. 'More . . . I'll give you mo—'

Her voice died abruptly. His body thrust upwards. He moaned as if in great pain, and then he felt himself flooded with sticky wetness and before he became ashamed of himself and his unbridled lust, he felt happier than he had ever felt before.

Now, as the *Seraph* sailed steadily southwards, almost motionless and sometimes eerily silent when submerged, and noisy and unruly when on the surface, her diesels going all out, he thought of that afternoon. But not only of the sexual pleasure she had given him with apparently nothing for herself save when she had allowed him to kiss her pert nipples, but of why she had done it.

She was not the 'minx' or 'hussy' of Mummy's fears. She had said she was still a virgin and he had believed her. Then why? In the end, as the *Seraph* slowly approached Gibraltar, he concluded she had given him so much pleasure because she had felt he was doomed, wasn't coming back. It was Wren Tidmus's gift to a man who was going to die . . .

Two

Slowly and very carefully Vice-Admiral Mercier drew on the skin-tight kid glove. Behind him Sergeant-Major Hans Hartmann, formerly of the French Legion d'Etranger, smiled, maliciously. The boss was going to start the business; he would finish it, no doubt, and enjoy every minute of it.

In the yellow light of the fly-specked naked bulb of the cell, the little sailor stared at the elegantly clad admiral – in his heavily gold-braided, immaculate white uniform – with some bewilderment. What had an admiral of the French Mediterranean Fleet got to do with him? Mercier would soon show him.

Mercier looked down at the skin-tight glove. He pursed his thick sensualist's lips. He, too, enjoyed these moments of tension, though he was not prepared to carry out the actual dirty business himself. What was going to happen next might well spoil his elegant uniform; he'd leave the nasty side to Hartmann. With his German thoroughness and usual brutality, he'd soon have the prisoner singing like a brave little yellow canary bird. After all, the German often boasted to his former comrades whenever he managed to return to the Bar de la Legion, where he, Mercier, had first found the scar-faced German exile, that 'I can make even a dirty mummy talk.'

Mercier pulled the glove even tighter, so that it fitted his elegantly manicured hand like a second skin, while the prisoner watched in fearful anticipation.

Suddenly, surprisingly, Mercier drew back his right hand and with all his strength reached out and slapped the little unshaven runt in his bloodstained shirt left and right across the face. The blow caught the prisoner completely off guard. He reeled back and forth and would have fallen if it had not

72

been for the concrete slab which served as a bunk and steadied him. '*Sale con!*' Mercier gasped through gritted teeth. '*Dites donc.*'

The prisoner righted himself. A thin trickle of dark blood started to flow from the side of his split mouth down the stubble of his chin. '*M'sleu l'Amiral,*' he whined, dabbing at the blood, eyes filled with tears of pain. 'I know nothing. *C'est vrai.*'

Mercier brought his face closer to that of the prisoner, nose wrinkled at the disgusting smell coming from the runt. He had already wet his baggy pants with fear. He'd do more before Hartmann had finished with him, especially if he weren't prepared to talk straight away. '*You lie!*' he hissed, eyes blazing with artificial fury. 'You have lied ever since you were taken.'

'No, I don't lie, sir,' the prisoner protested. 'I'm an honest fisherman from Marseilles, who got blown off course, sir. Honestly. I—'

'You are a damned spy for the English or that traitor de Gaulle,' Mercier cut him off brutally. Then he slapped the runt once more, saying, 'You'd better speak now, *salaud* . . . or it will be the worse for you. Down here –' he indicated the squalid cell, bare save for the concrete slab and the evil-smelling 'piss bucket', moisture trickling down its ancient stone walls – no one will hear your cries . . . Indeed, no one will notice if you disappear for ever and a day. Now it's up to you.' He nodded to Hartmann, eager to play his role in the interrogation.

The big Legion NCO needed no urging. He rolled up his sleeves, spat on the palms of his hands and picked up the piss bucket. Before the runt could react or even realize what was going to happen to him, he had slapped the stinking pail over the prisoner's head. Next moment he had raised the broom he had brought with him into the cell, his muscles rippling savagely beneath the tightness of his khaki shirt, and slammed it with all his strength against the pail.

The blow caught the runt completely off guard. He staggered against the wall, a muffled howl of pain coming from beneath the pail.

Mercier removed his glove carefully, as if it were important

to do so, saying to a panting Hartmann, *'Prima! Weiter so.'*
He spoke his native Alsatian German, Hartmann being one of
the few with whom he did so. Alsatians had never been popular
with the rest of France and especially with the French Navy.
The name Mercier was French enough and he had always kept
his Alsatian origin secret. But occasionally, in particular when
things were going well, he lapsed into his native tongue,
gaining some inner satisfaction, which he couldn't quite
explain, from doing so.

'Danke, Herr Admiral!' Hartmann said, and raised the
broom once again. *'Es wird nicht lange dauern* . . . The shit
heap has already pissed himself again.' He slammed the broom
against the pail and the prisoner shot backwards, blood
streaming down from beneath the bucket in bright-red rivulets.

Mercier touched his hand to his cap in a kind of a salute
and rattled the door for the warder to open it again. He had
seen enough of the sordid business.

Back in his big sunlit office overlooking Algiers' harbour,
Mercier pondered the situation in the capital this late summer's
day. On the whole, the situation was favourable for the German
occupiers and people like himself who supported the New
Order as something which would cleanse the old decadent
Europe of pre-1940 and deal with the red-Jewish rabble who
had ruined France once and for all.

The *'pieds-noirs'** – those who had been born in North
Africa but who considered themselves French and way above
the Arabs, those *'beni-beni-oui-ouis'*,† as they called the native
population contemptuously – seemed content with their lot.
Food was not difficult. They were making money, very important for them, and were – seemingly – totally unconcerned
with the fact that their country had been defeated in 1940 and
that the real masters of Algeria were now the German Control
Commission officers. Their only problem, it appeared to a now
thoughtful Mercier as he looked out at the calm blue surface
of the sea, shimmering a little in the heat, was the Arabs. They
were becoming difficult. They had seen their French masters

*'Black-feet', indicating they had native blood.
†Roughly, 'Sons of Yes-Yeses.'

defeated and disgraced by the Germans. Now they wanted rid of them so that they could regain their independence after nearly sixty years of being a French colony.

Carefully Mercier lit a cigarette and sucked in the smoke thoughtfully. But, naturally, in due course, they would deal with the Arabs. The Germans would support them even if it came to fighting. They, too, felt that the Arabs were an inferior people, just like the Jews. Perhaps the Germans would even set up those concentration camps of theirs which he had heard about, so that they could get rid of the Arabs more quickly.

But that would be in the future. His present problem was the handful of French locals, mostly from mainland France, both military and civilian, who supported that traitor de Gaulle in London, now under Vichy's sentence of death for desertion from the Army and treachery. Mercier pursed his lips, as he pondered the problem. He didn't think he'd have much of a problem with the military, who sided with the Free French. Most of the senior soldiers now in Algeria had been captured by the Germans back in 1940 and in order to be released from enemy captivity had given their soldiers' word of honour that they wouldn't fight against Germany in this war. Besides, all of them, ex-prisoners or otherwise, had sworn an oath of loyalty to the Vichy Government.

It was the civilian supporters of de Gaulle he was worried about. They could be anyone, from a businessman seemingly tamely working in his air-conditioned office in the French part of Algiers, to some shock-haired unshaven youth at the University of Algiers. It would be difficult to apprehend them. And they were getting support from the European mainland as well as locally. Someone, probably right here in Algiers, was supplying them with the money they needed for their pro-Free French agitation, and probably also with weapons.

He considered the prisoner down below, now being forced into a confession by Sergeant-Major Hartmann. He had been apprehended the day before in a small fishing boat which the local coastguard had observed dumping something over the side into the sea once the runt had spotted the coastguard cutter approaching him at top speed. The prisoner had probably been running guns for the insurgents; the second of his kind captured this last month. The questions now to be solved – who had paid for these guns and to whom were they being delivered? Solve those two questions, Mercier told himself thoughtfully, in particular the second one, and he would soon be wrapping up the whole damned Free French network in Algiers.

It was then that the admiral was distracted from his problem by the thin whine of an ambulance's siren, as the squat, box-like vehicle approached Intelligence Headquarters at speed.

Hurriedly he rose to his feet and crossed to the window which overlooked the street below. But before he could reach it, there was an urgent knocking at his door. Hurriedly he turned and snapped, '*Entrez!*'

It was Hartmann. He was sweating heavily and not looking as happy as he had been when Mercier had left him in the cell to carry out his cruel task. His big paws were red with blood too, the gobs of liquid dripping on Mercier's impeccable office floor.

A little annoyed by the sight, Mercier snapped, 'What is it, Sergeant-Major?'

'The little piss pansy went and frigging well died on me before I could get everything out of him. Yer can't trust little sods like that.' He breathed out hard like a man sorely tried. 'Must have hit him too hard, though he should have been able to stand a few whacks on his nut, the soft bastard.' He sighed again. 'They say his heart burst or something stupid—'

'What *did* you get out of him?' Mercier interrupted the big Legionnaire,

'He was working for them all right, de Gaulle's lot, sir, that was for sure.'

'I'd guessed that,' Mercier retorted impatiently. Sometimes these Germans were really slow and wooden-headed. How they had been able to beat France back in '40 he couldn't imagine. 'Anything else? His contact people here in Algiers for example.'

Hartmann brightened up a little. 'Before he snuffed it, sir, he babbled something about an *Ami* – an American.'

Marcier paused in mid-stride. 'What did you say?'

Hartmann repeated what he had just said.

76

Mercier's heart started to race abruptly. 'An American,' he said. 'What kind of an American?'

Hartmann shrugged. 'Just an American, sir,' he answered. 'The prisoner was to rendezvous with him at the cathedral. That's about it, sir.' He wiped the blood off his right hand and looked at his partially clean hand as if it was of some significance. Then he added, 'We might find out more when we check through his duds, sir, and we could have another look at that boat of his . . .' His voice trailed away to nothing. He could see that the admiral wasn't listening to him. He shrugged slightly. What did it matter to him? Let the Frogs get on with their silly feuds and the like. He'd sit out the war here in North Africa and then, once he was eligible for French citizenship and a Legion pension, he'd return to France, find a young tart and live off the earnings of the 'pavement pounder'. It was a better future than having your throat slit by some towelhead, high on hashish and religion, or your head blown off by a Russki in the godforsaken wastes of Russia with the German *Wehrmacht*.

'An American, who might be a Catholic,' Mercier was musing to himself, as outside now the ambulance men were carrying out the dead runt on a stretcher, the blood dropping in ugly red gobs on the pavement as they did so. Although America still maintained diplomatic relations with the Vichy Government, there were few Americans left in Algiers. They were mostly hopeful, aggressive salesmen for the big armanent companies, prepared to risk an embargo on the export of such goods, and trying to sell their planes and guns to an antiquated French Army in Africa. But Mercier guessed not many of this handful of Americans would be Catholic – he guessed 'Mr X', as he was now calling the dead prisoner's American contact, was one. Why else would he meet the dead runt in such a place? Most Americans, he told himself, would make contact in one of the more expensive bars in the capital's French Quarter. In his experience, Americans, as prudish and puritain as they usually were, were also great boozers – not that they could hold their alcohol.

Abruptly he broke his silence. 'All right, Hartmann, go and get yourself cleaned up. We've – you've – got a job.'

77

'What's that, sir?'

'To find an *Ami*, as you call them.'

Hartmann looked puzzled. 'What kind of an *Ami*, sir?'

'One who is Catholic, got plenty of money, and seems to have contacts with those traitors we know work with de Gaulle.'

Hartmann forced a laugh. 'Bit of a tall order, sir.' He risked a joke. He knew that while most people feared Mercier, he knew too much about the admiral, especially his taste in under-age girls, to be scared. He said, 'Would you like me to find out if this American has a mole on his left buttock, anything like that, sir?'

Admiral Mercier didn't seem to hear; he was too preoccupied with his problem. He waved his hand and it was clear to Hartmann that it was time to go. He saluted awkwardly, the dead man's blood running down his wrist. Moments later the big, shaven-headed German was swallowed up by the noise and squalor of the baking capital.

Three

'*General – the light!*' Jewell called down the conning tower of HMS *Seraph* urgently.

Hastily Clark, who had been knocked black and blue during the voyage from Gibraltar, trying to accommodate his six-foot-three-inch frame to the tight confines of the submarine, clambered up the ladder from below, glad to escape its hot fetid atmosphere and the knobs everywhere. Behind him, Smythe and the SBS officers, already dressed in their camouflage smocks, waited tensely for their orders. Even Sambo Simpson was silent and in no mood to crack his usual jokes.

They had been sailing two days now, mostly below the surface to avoid the Vichy French and German patrol boats which seemed to be everywhere off the North African coast. Even Jewell had been caught off guard in Gibraltar when the 'Yanks' had appeared the night they had sailed. Not only were there four of them, including a full captain in the US Navy, but the general he had expected turned out to be a Mark Wayne Clark, Deputy Supreme Commander in London and the future commander in the field of the US Fifth Army.

But there had been no time to wonder at the unexpected high-ranking US officer who was going to conduct secret talks with the French. Time was running out, for Clark let it be known that the convoys carrying the invaders to North Africa were already beginning to sail. Their voyage would be long but by the time they arrived at their designated invasion beaches, Clark wanted the French to have laid down their arms and offer no resistance to the Anglo-American armies.

Now they were there, thanks to Jewell and his veterans, two miles off the coast of Algeria. The white light gleaming from a height just above the deserted moonlit shore – the signal agreed upon previously by General Mast and his French Army plotters – telling them that the coast was clear. Soon the SBS, navigated by a nervous, worried Smythe, could start landing their 'Yank'.

There was no time to be lost, Smythe knew that. The submarine was at its most vulnerable here in the shallow water of the lonely bay, only two miles out, in easy reach of any artillery their Franco-German enemies might bring up. And in the event of an attack from the air, the water wouldn't be deep enough for the *Seraph* to submerge successfully.

Now, once Churchill's 'American Eagle' seemed satisfied that everything was going as planned, Jewell gave the order for Smythe and the SBS officers to launch the folboats. These were very light craft made of wood and canvas, which were easy to carry but damnably difficult to manage in rough water of the kind they would soon be facing once they had left the sub.

Finally they got them over the side and, trying not to overturn the frail little boats, the officers of Clark's staff followed their commander to board them. Clark – naturally – took his place in Smythe's leading boat, where he now gave the whispered order, 'Take 'em away, Lieutenant. Stop at every two hundred yards so that we can check that everything is all right.'

'Yessir,' the young officer replied, well aware of his responsibility in carrying such a senior US officer. If he lost Clark, a little voice at the back of his head warned, they'd probably imprison him in the Tower of London for the rest of his born days.

Swiftly Smythe formed his little group into a 'V' formation, with his own folboat at the point of the 'V'. The surf caught the frail craft at once and although Smythe was used to 'mucking about in small boats', he found it difficult to keep his on course, paddling furiously and switching rapidly from left to right as the rushing white water threatened to throw him off course more than once. Behind him, Clark moaned, 'Holy cow, what an SOB this is.' Ignoring the moaned complaint, Smythe continued paddling, aware that once the water forced him off course, he might well miss the entrance to the bay and the rendezvous altogether.

But, as Clark snapped above the hiss and thrust of the surf, 'Two hundred yards,' and he and the SBS focused their glasses the best they could on the distant shore, they were still on course. They set off again. But even as he paddled in the lead, Smythe told himself that it was all going too easily, apart from the problem presented by the water. If anyone was there to greet them, he was keeping himself well under cover. Why? Perhaps someone they had not expected was lying in wait for them and they were heading straight into a trap . . . And Smythe knew what would happen then if he fell into the hands of the Germans. Even though all of the landing party were in uniform, he didn't doubt for one minute that the enemy would put them up against the nearest wall and shoot them out of hand.

He dismissed that particularly unpleasant thought and concentrated on the paddling as, behind him, Clark, his long legs in the way, prepared to count off the next two hundred yards.

In the end they stopped at the last 200 yards, the paddlers already breathing hard and feeling the strain, their shoulder muscles burning as if someone had just prodded them with a red-hot poker. Now they could see the rendezvous more clearly. All was silent on the beach, the only real noise the sad howling of a dog a long way off and the slither-and-hiss of the pebbles as they were swept back and forth by the force of the brilliant white surf.

Smythe threw a glance at his watch. It was nearly midnight. Someone should have made contact by now. He peered through the silver gloom of the half moon over Africa. The naked bulb which had been their guiding light so far was placed in the dormer window of what looked like a farmhouse: it lay on the cliff top, a structure of stucco walls and a red mansard roof. No sign of life came from it.

Then suddenly and startlingly on the beach below came the dash-dot-dash of the letter 'K' in the morse code. It was the all-clear signal. Smythe grabbed his paddle once more and signalled by hand to Sambo Simpson, who was carrying Colonel Holmes of the US Army as his passenger, to take the lead.

Swiftly the big SBS soldier did so, skimming neatly over the remaining breakers to the shore as his passenger pulled out his colt pistol in readiness for any trouble.

Minutes later the three Englishmen and their American passengers were dragging up their boats through the wet sand ready to hide them in the black shadows cast by the bushes at the foot of the bluff. Suddenly they tensed. A dark figure had detached itself from the clump of trees to their left. The Americans raised their .45s while General Clark levelled his carbine. Abruptly their hands were damp with sweat. Their hearts beat furiously. Was this a trap after all?

Colonel Holmes rose cautiously to his feet. He was the only one of the party who had ever met the head of the reception committee personally. He levelled his pistol and clicked off the safety as a man stepped out of the trees into the moonlight. To Smythe, the metallic sound felt as if it might well be heard all the way to Berlin.

Out of the olive trees emerged a tall, stooped, middle-aged man, wearing a turtleneck sweater, sneakers and a typical American baseball cap.

Holmes lowered his pistol immediately. 'Bob!' he cried, advancing on the lone American, hand outstretched. '*Bob Murphy!*' Holmes, who had worked with Murphy before the war, could not fail to recognize the US State Department's most senior diplomat in North Africa, who was also the head of the Franco-American spy ring in Algiers.

Behind him, lying in the wet sand, carbine at the ready, Clark breathed a sigh of relief. Contact had been made at last. Moments later the new arrivals were surrounded by the other conspirators, French and American, having their backs slapped excitedly, while Smythe and the two SBS officers waited on the fringes, impatient to have their precious American charges under cover.

Now Murphy, the arch-plotter, who had been working to arrange this kind of meeting for weeks, perhaps months, turned to General Clark. He held out his hand. This was an historic moment, but at that particular moment neither the civilian nor the soldier knew just how historic. For this was the first time in American history that the USA was going to capriciously enter into the affairs of an independent Middle-Eastern country – it wouldn't be the last time, however. 'General,' he said simply. 'Welcome to North Africa!'

Clark wasn't equal to that moment of history. He abandoned the speech he had prepared in French, and growled simply, 'I'm damned glad we made it . . .'

Thereafter things moved swiftly.

Clark's first problem was to hide the three British. Not only was he worried about the Vichy French, he was also concerned that General Mast, who he was to meet soon, wouldn't even begin talks on Franco-American co-operation on the day of the Anglo-American invasion if he knew Britons were present; the memory of the massacre of the French fleet at Mers-el-Kebir was too fresh. Although the British Army was going to form the major part of that invasion, Clark wanted the French to believe that the attack was going to be 100 per cent American. In the end he decided to put them in the white-painted colonial farmhouse on the top of the cliff owned by a nervous Monsieur Teissier, a patriot who knew he was risking not only his freedom but perhaps also his life by helping the Americans. For there were spies everywhere on that key stretch of coastline near to the capital Algiers: French agents spying for de Gaulle, unreliable and given to too much boasting; Vichy Frenchmen and Arabs working for their own factions – and anybody else prepared to pay them.

The blood-red ball of the sun was slipping over the horizon to the east when they heard the sound of motors on the road from Algiers. They indicated that General Mast and his staff were on their way for the key talks. Clark warned his staff that they must not reveal to the French the actual date of the invasion. That was to remain top secret to the very last, even if Mast agreed to help the invaders. For now the Americans had at last learned that French security was lousy. They simply could not be trusted to keep a secret.

Now the English moved into the Teissier farmhouse and were ordered to keep out of sight at all costs. 'Great balls of fire,' Sambo complained, 'We're like bloody spectres at the feast. Who the bloody hell do those Yanks think we are?'

Smythe felt the same, but he reasoned he was too young

and inexperienced to voice his thoughts in front of these older men. Instead he lay down on the hard floor, pulling his blanket over him in the same instant that one of Teissier's Arab servants appeared, bearing a large bottle of scotch on a silver tray.

Sambo brightened up immediately. He stroked his impressive moustache, wet his lips and chortled, 'Well, it's not going to be that bad nursemaiding these Yanks after all – as long as they don't wet their knickers too often. Pass me that bottle, my man.'

Unfortunately the Yanks *were* really going to wet their knickers before this long day was over.

Four

At six that morning, with the sun warming the chilled fields and indicating that it was going to be another splendid early autumn day, General Mast and his staff officers arrived in civilian cars instead of their usual immaculate command cars, which would have identified them immediately as Army officers.

Mast, short, burly and fluent in English, had escaped from a German POW camp in 1940. But he had not lost his will to fight, and although he had signed an oath of loyalty to the pro German Vichy Government, he was now prepared to support the Americans when they invaded North Africa. He would ensure that his own 19th Infantry Corps would not oppose their landings and, given time, so he later told Clark, he would bring the rest of the army and air force in Algeria over to the American cause. Thereafter he was prepared to take on the Germans, who would undoubtedly rush troops from Rommel's front to stop the US assault.

Now, after a brisk exchange of salutes and the usual diplomatic small talk, he and Clark, supported by Murphy, the senior State Department official in French North Africa, got down to business over a dish of olives and small glasses of sickly sweet wine. They talked for four hours, telling each other what were essentially lies.

Mast, on the verge of weeping at times about the state of the French Army in Algeria, said he would be able to raise an army of 300,000 troops, which was his first lie, and then North Africa would 'flame into revolt', his second lie. But he needed American arms to do so, and time.

Clark replied vaguely, for he was under orders from President Roosevelt himself not to tell the small French general that the Americans were going to invade a lot sooner than Mast anticipated. 'It's best to do something soon. We have the army and the means.'

Mast asked how big this army was going to be. Clark replied that the US Army would consist of a half a million men and two thousand aircraft. That was *his* first lie.

As Teissier started to serve breakfast – coffee and sardines on flat unleaven Arab bread – Mast asked, 'Where are these five hundred thousand men to come from? Where are these troops now?'

'In the US and UK,' Clark replied.

'Rather far, isn't it?'

'No,' Clark said bluntly. And that was his second lie.

By the time that Mast was ready to return to his headquarters, the seeds of confusion and distrust had been sown between the two would-be allies. They concerned the timing of the invasion; who was to command the Allied armies, if they were to include the French Army in Africa and take charge of the three French colonies if the German Control Commission and the Vichy administrators were driven out. By eleven o'clock, Mast had had enough. He stood up and said he'd better get back to Algiers before his absence was noted. But before walking to his car, he warned Clark, flushed by so much talk and quick lying, 'The French Navy is not with me. The Army and Air Force are.'

Clark began to relax. Monsieur Teissier, worried and nervous, served his visitors, including a few of Mast's staff officers who had stayed behind, a lunch of red-hot peppery chicken, red wine and oranges. While the Mast Officers handed over top secret maps of defensive positions, airfields, troop strengths etc to Clark's officers, the tall rangy 'American Eagle' borrowed an ill-fitting uniform blouse from one of the French officers and went outside for a stroll and some fresh air.

But he was not going to enjoy his time out of war for long. Suddenly, inside the house the telephone began to ring urgently, disturbing the morning calm. Teissier just managed not to drop the tray of drinks – he was that nervous. He sprang to the phone. '*Mon Dieu!*' he gasped as he listened to the unknown person at the end of the line. Next moment he slammed the phone down with a hand that shook wildly. He cried, 'Gentlemen, the police will be here in five minutes.'

Clark, just outside the open window, heard him. Before he could react, one of Mast's officers bolted out of the door, carrying his briefcase with the top-secret documents. Other French dived through the window and fled into the bushes. 'Restez là, for God's sake!' Clark yelled, as he picked up the noise of motors in the far distance. To no avail. The French officers were overwhelmed with panic.

Clark's own officers were little better. Here they were, clad in US Army uniform, four thousand miles or so away from the States. How would they be able to explain that to the French cops? Hurriedly, as they, too, prepared to flee, Clark's officers started to divest themselves of the bribes they had brought with them from Gibraltar. Dollars, Canadian gold pieces, greasy bundles of worthless French francs rained down on a shocked Murphy. He was a diplomat, accredited in Algiers, and a civilian, who knew the Frogs and could speak fluent French. Perhaps he could grease the palms of the French cops to look the other way. At all events, they didn't want to be arrested with all that dough on them; it would be a dead giveaway.

Clark pulled himself together. He took charge as the French officers on Mast's staff tumbled into their civilian car and set off up the steep hill with a squeal of burning rubber. 'Murphy, see if you can hold 'em off for a while. I've got to get my guys out of here, pronto.' Leaving the diplomat to get on with it, he called to the three Britishers, 'Get into the wine cellar – quick, for God's sake!'

They needed no urging, and as the American officers left Murphy, Teissier and a lone French officer to attempt to stall the police, whose car was now in view, they filed into the cellar, dragging their folboats with them. A bit later Clark and his officers joined them. Hearts thumping wildly, they crouched there in the half-darkness, their nostrils filled with the heavy smell of red wine, while, outside, the police car braked to a stop and they could hear the heavy stamp of cops' boots as they spread out to search the cliff-top farmhouse.

In the living room, Murphy and the other two Frenchmen had hurriedly surrounded themselves with spirits and bottles of wine. Their glasses were already filled and as the police sergeant came in, followed by his Arab assistants and informers – the Arabs thought they'd get a reward from the French authorities for having reported what they thought was a smuggling operation – they raised their glasses to the suspicious sergeant in what appeared a drunken toast. '*A votre santé, M'sieu le Commissaire* . . . We're having a party.'

Murphy, the staid formal Catholic diplomat, managed a stage wink and added, 'Soon the naughty girls will arrive . . . You understand, M'sieu?'

'Some girls – good wine and a little food,' a trembling Teissier added shakily.

The sergeant grunted something and turned away to direct the search team, while Teissier clutched his flies hurriedly, as if he were in the sudden throes of sexual passion. In truth he felt he was going to wet himself with fright.

In the cellar they waited tensely. Clark was fiddling with his carbine, as if he were ready to shoot it out Texan-style if the worst came to the worst, clicking the mechanism up and down and muttering, 'How in Sam Hill's name does this goddam thing work?'

'For God's sake,' Ferguson snapped, losing patience with the general. 'Put the damned thing down.'

Just then Sambo was seized by a fit of coughing. His comrades and the Americans tensed. The police searchers were only yards away; they could hear the squawk-squawk of Teissier's chickens as they scattered them. The big SBS soldier stuttered, 'General, I'm afraid I'm going to choke, sir.'

Clark didn't hesitate. 'I'm afraid you won't,' he said. He slipped a wad of chewing gum into Sambo's mouth. The latter responded, once his coughing had subsided, with, 'This chewing gum doesn't seem to have much taste, sir.'

Clark replied, 'I'm not surprised, Captain. I've just been chewing it myself to calm my nerves.'

Now they waited in tense silence till they heard the grind of two cars making their way up the steep hill in low gear. Minutes later there was a hoarse whisper from above. It was

Murphy. 'They've gone for the time being . . . but we think they'll be back.'

'How long?' Clark snapped hurriedly.

'Just a little while, Wayne. Better clear the house.'

'Wilco.'

Clark knew it was time to get back to the *Seraph*, lying somewhere offshore. He had carried out the dangerous mission, for which he knew he had to be given another medal, perhaps from the hands of the President himself. That would mean another star in due course. Now he knew it would serve no purpose if he were captured by the French police. They were in the pay of Vichy and there'd be one holy hell of a stink if they were to reveal they had captured American officers dressed in US uniforms on French territory, even if France was now a neutral. It would be even worse if they handed over American prisoners to the German Control Commission in Algiers. First the Gestapo would work them over and then in due course they'd be quietly bumped off. 'All right, fellows,' he commanded, 'let's get out of here while it's safe.'

The others needed no urging. Gathering their weapons and their kit, they crept up the ladder from the cellar and went outside. It was already dark, but still they could see that the stiff wind which was now blowing was whipping up the waves into an angry white frenzy. Time and time again the recognition signal from the submarine, which seemed about a mile from the beach, was obscured by the tide. Still Clark knew they had to chance the power of the surf.

Together with Sambo he entered the water. Immediately he felt it surging around his lower body, trying to knock him over. He wasn't helped either by the fact that he was weighed down and hampered by the weight of the several score of gold coins and wads of dollar bills which packed the money belt around his waist.

Clark, steadied a little by Sambo, now tried to board the frail wood and canvas folboat, which bobbed up and down alarmingly as the current tried to topple him and Clark over. Finally, after what seemed an age, the two of them, now completely soaked, managed to scramble their way aboard. But not for long. A moment later a huge wave crashed down upon them. The folboat overturned. Next instant they were coughing and spluttering and trying to stand upright in the swirling cauldron of angry foam, the general without his trousers.

The others plunged in to rescue them. Ferguson cried in that angry Ulster voice of his, 'Never mind the General . . . For heaven's sake get the damned paddles.' They did so and moments later they were making their way back to the cover of a little grove of stunted olive trees further up the beach, where they considered their position. Murphy sent word that the gendarmes had not returned. They were still searching the area. Clark made a decision; he didn't want to face that damned ice-cold surf again. He dispatched the remaining French officer to the village to bribe an Arab fisherman to take them out to the still waiting submarine. The Arab refused; it was too dangerous, even though the French officer offered him gold coins for the task.

Clark now lost confidence. He started to grasp at straws. First he radioed the *Seraph* to stand by at an agreed time to take them off if they could manage to get that far. Then he thought they might be able to bribe someone to find them travel papers and a car which would take them across the border to Spanish Morocco to the west. In the end he decided against it and told himself that it was his first priority to get some dry clothes before he did anything.

Monsieur Teissier nearly fell out of his chair when he saw the general, soaked to the skin, his hair rumpled and still dripping water. He thought he had got rid of him and the others for good. Now here was the big American, speaking broken French, wanting clothes and drink. He tried to get rid of Clark. To no avail.

Clark insisted he was going to stay until he got what he wanted. Clark got his way. He was just stuffing two bottles of red wine into his tight sweater when there was the sound of a car engine. It was the French police returning. Now Clark waited no longer. He dropped ten feet over a sea wall. He yelped with pain as the sharp pebbles cut his bare feet. But although he lost the loaf of bread, he managed to save the red wine.

Finally, at three in the morning, the gendarmes completed their second search and departed. But, as they relaxed, the mixed group of Britons and Americans could see that the sea was still raging. There had been no change. But it was Sambo who came up with a bright idea. 'I say, chaps,' he commenced in that very English manner of his, as if he had all the time in the world to chat. 'Once when I was on the Gold Coast—'

'Oh, put a sock in it, Sambo,' Ferguson cut in hastily, while Smythe watched, wondering what the Yanks must have thought of these two big British officers.

Sambo wasn't listening. 'Well, out there I watched how the blackies got their boats out when the surf was rough.'

Clark suddenly showed interest. 'Go on,' he urged, taking a slug of the red wine straight from the bottle.

'Well, sir, they carried their boats out over the first line of surf, the most dangerous part. There they held it steady until some of their black pals clambered aboard.'

'We'll try it,' Clark decided. 'Hell, we haven't got any alternative.'

What followed was a tremendous battle between man and nature. Time and time again, just as they had steadied one of the frail folboats, a great wave came gushing in in white fury and overturned it. But still they persisted, soaked and gasping for breath, feeling sick with the amount of sea water. Four lights on the cliff above indicated that either the police were returning, or worse, the Vichy French and their German masters.

Smythe, who knew he didn't have the strength of the two SBS officers, made up his mind. He slipped back and wiped his sten gun hurriedly. Then he clambered on to the shore and knelt, little automatic at the ready. He'd hold off whoever it was till the others had reached the *Seraph*, then he'd swim for it. It wasn't till the tracer slugs from above cut the morning darkness in a stream of lethal white morse that he realized what a bloody young fool he was.

Five

Clark slid down the ladder from the conning tower, soaked and panting, still clutching the last bottle of red wine to his chest, as if it were very precious. 'We've lost some bags with important documents,' he gasped to Commander Jewell. 'We ought to try and dive and find them.'

Jewell shook his head firmly. His ship and its crew were more important to him than documents, no matter how precious they were. 'Can't do it, sir. You can see, sir, it's getting very light. We'd better submerge before the Frogs on the cliff spot us, sir.'

Clark gave in. He had had enough of the current and the damned surf. He was almost exhausted. He said, 'OK, skipper, you're the boss.'

Jewell nodded, as if he agreed with the US general that he really was the boss.

Hurriedly he ordered the klaxons sounded to indicate the boat was going to dive. They screeched their warning, drowning the sound of small-arms fire from the shore.

As the hatch of the conning tower clanked down and Jewell's number one took over the bridge, Clark slumped, all energy drained from him as if a tap had been abruptly opened. He said to Jewell, still dripping sea water. 'You know, Commander, the US Navy is dry. No booze allowed on board. I hear, however, that your majesty's Royal Navy is wet.'

Behind him, Sambo as good-humoured as ever, despite what they had just been through, cracked, 'You can say that again, sir. Very wet indeed.'

Jewell froze him with a look and said, 'You're right there, sir. Nelson's blood and splice the mainbrace and all that. But in subs, sir, we only take a tot of rum in emergencies.'

Clark gave him his craggy-faced grin. 'Well, this *is* an emergency – at least, it is for me. I need a goddam strong drink. So, as I outrank you by far, Commander, I'm going to declare this an emergency and order a double rum ration for all aboard the *Seraph*.' From the rear of the submarine where the torpedo mates stood behind their weapons, there came a cheer.

'Yessir,' Jewell said. 'I suppose you have the rank to sign the emergency order.'

'I think I have,' Clark answered with a grin.

Jewell turned round to face the senior petty officer on board. 'All right, Chiefie, splice the mainbrace.'

This time the crew was not intimidated by the presence of the US general. As the chief petty officer dragged out the highly polished brass-bound barrel which contained the precious rum, they cheered.

Gratefully, and still grinning, Churchill's 'American Eagle' raised the first tot served by the CPO and said, in toast, 'Here's to the success of the new operation. Here's to the future success of HMS *Seraph* and all such Anglo-American ops.'

As one, the happy crew members raised their mugs. It was then that they discovered, after the CPO had carefully counted out the tots as regulations required, that one member of the party had not claimed his rum. It was Lieutenant Horatio Smythe . . .

Smythe awoke with a groan. For a moment he dared not move. He felt that if he did his aching head might well fall off. But then the persistent drip-drip caught his imagination and he opened his eyes. He was confronted by bare concrete walls, a barred window high up above him, a pail and a hole in the floor which would be the latrine, a battered three-legged stool and the concrete block upon which he now lay. He licked his parched, cracked lips and muttered to himself, 'Bloody hell – a cell.'

As if to confirm his conclusion, there came the muffled sound of chains outside and the clatter of keys against each door in the corridor. It was obviously some warder escorting a shackled prisoner, alerting each cell member with the rattle of those keys to keep his head down and not look into the corridor.

Smythe groaned again. This time it was not with pain, but with dismay. Suddenly it all came flooding back and he remembered what had happened on that wild, windswept beach – and the memory was not pleasant. In the dirty white light of the false dawn, he had seen the cops, if they were cops, beginning to thread their way down the zig-zagging cliff path, and he had known that in minutes they'd discover him down there on the beach. Beyond, they'd see the *Seraph*, and then, he guessed, all hell would be let loose. For what seemed a long time he had hesitated. It was not every day, after all, that he had to make the decision to fire on his fellow human beings and possibly kill them.

'*Los!*' the cry came from above, and although he was no linguist, Smythe recognized the command as German and not French. That single word made up his mind for him. He pressed the trigger of the little automatic, remembering even at this moment of extreme tension to keep his little finger out of the way of the little slot from which the cartridge cases were ejected, as he had been taught to. If he didn't, he'd soon be minus a small finger.

The sten erupted against his hip bone. The sea air was abruptly filled with the acrid stink of burned cordite. A series of angry blue sparks erupted on the cliff above him. Somebody yelled out in pain. There was the clatter of a weapon falling to the ground and then violet flame stabbed the gloom as the supposed cops began returning his fire. Bullets gouged up the sand all about him. But Smythe seemed to bear a charmed life, or the enemy were rotten shots. They missed time and time again.

Smythe told himself he'd done enough, he'd stalled the descent of the 'cops' for a while. Now it was time to hoof it to the others, who were hidden at the other side of the cove as they attempted to launch their frail craft into the roaring, noisy surf, so that they probably could not hear the angry snap-and-crack of the small-arms fight. He rose and, in a half crouch, he loosed quick bursts to left and right like some western gunslinger in the cowboy films he had enjoyed so much as a kid.

But now the pursuers were rising to their feet and advancing cautiously, firing as they came. Now their fire was more accurate. A sweating Smythe was tempted to run for it while he still had chance. But he thought of his comrades and, in particular, of the American general, who seemed so awkward and clumsy in boats. He had to give them and him a fair chance. Not that he had any idea of self-sacrifice. But he was a very strong swimmer and he reasoned, once he was through the surf, he had a pretty good chance of reaching HMS *Seraph*, which was only a mile away.

But Horatio Smythe was not fated to reach the submarine. As he backed off, still firing though he sensed the sten's magazine was getting very low on ammunition, he stumbled on a concealed boulder. Wildly he tried to regain his balance. To no avail. He went down, the sten tumbling from his hands. Next moment a giant in the white kepi of the Foreign Legion seemed to appear from nowhere.

Desperately Smythe grabbed for the sten gun. The giant Legionnaire beat him to it. He aimed a tremendous kick at the weapon. He sent it scudding across the sand, its magazine falling off as it did so. Then, for good measure, crying '*Arsehole, enough!*' he followed up the first kick with another aimed directly at the young officer's head. That did it. Bright silver stars exploded in front of Smythe's bulging eyes. Next moment a blood-red veil had descended upon him and he had known no more.

Smythe moaned again as he remembered what had happened next after he had regained consciousness to find himself bundled in the back of a big smelly Citroën, his hands bound cruelly behind his back, his head throbbing painfully. Next to him sat the big man in the white kepi who had knocked him unconscious. As the little convoy of supposed policemen made its way back to Algiers, the man had sat there drinking and smoking moodily until another man sitting next to the driver rapped out something in German. The big man put away his flask of arak immediately and snapped, '*Jawohl, Herr Admiral.*' That much Smythe had understood, and had felt a sinking sensation as he assumed he had fallen into the hands of the Germans, even though his captors were wearing French uniform. But even at this moment of fear, the young British officer wondered why a German admiral should be involved in a police raid like the one at the farmhouse on the cliff.

But he had no time to consider the matter further, as the brute of a man in the white kepi dug him cruelly in the ribs and demanded, '*Alors, que fais tu dans la ferme? Responds, sale con.*' Smythe's French dated back to his days in prep school and a few lessons in naval French at Dartmouth. Still he realized that his interrogator's accent was not French and his French language was pretty ungrammatical. Again this confirmed his belief that somehow he had fallen into the hands of the Huns. Remembering his training at Dartmouth, he answered tight-lipped, '*Ne comprends pas.*' He thought that was the best way to deal with questions for the time being.

The response of the man in the white kepi was immediate. He slammed his fist into Smythe's face and growled, 'Don't worry, comrade. I'll soon have you singing like a bird.' He reached into his pocket hastily and pulled out something which Smythe recognized in the poor light at the back of the car as brass knuckles. He pulled back his muscular arm once more and hissed gleefully, 'Now try this, comrade.' But before he could launch the punch which might well have knocked out all Smythe's front teeth, the man he had addressed as 'Herr Admiral' commanded in French, '*Ça suffit . . . plus tard, hein?*'

And that had been that. They had continued the rest of their journey to the Algerian capital in a gloomy, leaden silence, tinged with fearful anticipation.

Now as he raised himself slowly, feeling the wave of pain sweep through his head, Smythe attempted to take stock of his situation. From what he had seen and heard before he had passed out a second time, the young officer guessed that he wasn't in German hands after all. His jail was French; he had been able to tell that from the language of the warders and the trustees, in their ragged striped pyjama-like uniform.

Naturally, his captors would soon discover that he was not only English but also a Royal Navy officer as well. Once the camouflage smock had been taken away from him, they'd realize that. What would be his ploy then? It was obvious that they knew that something fishy had been going on in the house

96

on the cliff. M'sieu Teissier had told him after the first lot of supposed policemen had disappeared that he suspected he had been betrayed by one of his Arab servants who had hoped for a reward by telling the Algiers authorities that his master had been engaged in some sort of illegal smuggling operation. But how could that explain why the policemen had returned to the remote house on the cliffs later? Or the presence of the big man in the white kepi who spoke fluent German and who wasn't a policeman, but, to judge from his uniform, a member of the French Army?

Smythe shook his head in bewilderment and wished the next moment he hadn't. The pain made him more acutely aware of the danger of his position, and that he had to have his cover story ready soon, before the French came to interrogate him. He was not afraid that they would physically harm him; after all, Britain was not at war with Vichy France. Even if he was on French territory dressed in British uniform, they couldn't regard him as a spy and shoot him out of hand like the Germans could. What was worrying, however, was this connection with the German enemy. To assist the Germans, his French captors might resort to torture to make him reveal what little he knew of the *Seraph*'s mission.

How would he be able to stand up to that? He didn't know. Suddenly Horatio Smythe, the 'young hero', as Commander Jewell had called him at their first meeting, felt very frightened. Not for himself, but for the others and the many thousands whom he suspected would be soon following them to Africa. Would he be able to keep his mouth shut and not betray them? Even as he heard the echo of the heavy boots in the stone-flagged corridor outside, and the clatter of a warder's keys, which indicated that they were coming to fetch him, Smythe felt more afraid than he had ever done since he had gone on active service . . .

Six

Outside in the prison's courtyard, a miserable bunch of deportees were being assembled to be escorted to the docks for shipment to France under the superivision of gendarmes swinging clubs and men of the Foreign Legion armed with rifles. They were the usual bunch of no-goods, Mercier thought, smoking fitfully through his long ivory cigarette holder. De Gaullist traitors, Jews, deserters from the Legion, a handful of Arab rebels and the like. Once they reached Marseilles on the mainland, the Germans would take over and they would disappear into the French concentration camps which the Germans and Vichy had established together, or be sent to the Reich to work in the German War Industry as France's contribution to the 'New Order' in Europe.

Mercier sniffed and told himself good riddance. The sooner France was cleared of such worthless trash, the better it would be for the 'New France' that would emerge after the war. Even if they were maintaining in Berlin that there would be something called the 'European Community' under the leadership of a victorious Third Reich, he knew eventually France would emerge to take that 'Community' over. In the end, France always triumphed over the greatest of adversities. Mercier had no doubt about that.

Standing at ease near the door of Mercier's office, Hartmann cleared his throat noisily. It was nearly midday and it was his custom to go over to one of the cheap bars that lined the waterfront, enjoy a few Ricards to get himself in the right mood, and then enjoy one of the whores who worked such places. It was an almost daily custom and Sergeant-Major Hartmann always thought that a day without a whore was a day misspent. As he told his old cronies of the Bar de la Legion, 'A man who don't get his dick daily, comrades, is only half a man. I'd venture to say that a man like that needs watching. I wouldn't be surprised if he wasn't a warm brother, comrades.' And he usually guffawed here at his own supposed humour, showing his great slab-like teeth and the one gold one he possessed, of which he was inordinately proud.

Slowly Mercier stubbed out his cigarette. Hartmann was right. They'd better get started on the Teissier business. It was puzzling, but, he guessed, somehow significant. How, he didn't exactly know. But it was his business to find out.

He tugged his elegantly manicured forefinger, the nail shining with nail varnish. 'The Gaullist –' he meant Teissier – 'has fled. 'So we have the Arab and this young fellow down below.'

'The towelhead knows nothing,' Hartmann said. 'I've questioned him.' He blew on his knuckles, to indicate how. 'He thinks Teissier was engaged in smuggling.'

'Yes, Hartmann. Very strange people who arrive in a submarine.' He smiled thinly. 'Not the usual manner of smugglers, yes?'

'Agreed, Admiral.'

'So we have to concentrate on the prisoner. What do you make of him, Hartmann?'

'Soft as shit, sir. Foreigner. Not kosher at all.' He rapped out his thoughts as if he were still back on the square as a drill curporal at the Legion fort of Sidi-bel-Abbes.

Mercier absorbed the information. Outside, one of the guards was clubbing a deportee who lay on the ground, trying to protect his testicles from the beating, blood pouring down his swarthy face. To judge from his '*Locken*', Mercier guessed he was an orthodox Jew. He nodded his approval and turned back to the big NCO. 'So, my dear Hartmann,' he asked, 'what do we do, eh?'

'We make the bastard sing, sir, and then take it from there.'

'*D'accord.*'

'Do we – er – knock him about, sir?'

'No, he looks pretty frail to me. Don't want the young man dying on us, do we?'

'It's all the same to me, sir.' Hartmann shrugged. 'Lot o' piss pansies, all of 'em.'

'No, let's humiliate him. Strip him naked. That always does the trick. Bring one of your whores in if you like. Let her make fun of his – er – appendages. Men don't like that.'

Hartmann grinned abruptly. 'Well, if I may say so, sir, after a piece of gash has seen me in the buff, even a whore, every other man looks a bit weedy in comparison, if you follow my meaning.'

'I do,' Mercier said coldly. The big German's words reminded him of his own failings, which had led him to the potential blackmail trap of young girls, virgins mostly, who were impressed by their first sight of the male organ, however small it might be. Naturally he knew that his tastes in that direction could lead to complications, serious complications, especially for a person of his rank and position. But it was a chance he had to take, if he were going to get any sexual pleasure at all. He forgot his own problems and said, 'You'd better start working on him straight away, Hartmann. Find out who he is, what his connection with Teissier is and what the devil he was doing out there in the first place. Don't knock him about too much. Otherwise you have carte blanche to do anything you like . . . I want a preliminary report by this evening. All right, Hartmann, dismiss.'

Hartmann sprang momentarily to attention, big chin thrust out, head raised, hands stretched rigidly down the sides of his khaki pants, heels clicked together. Mercier told himself that the ex-sergeant-major of the Foreign Legion was a typical German thug. But he was a useful one. Such Germans had brutal talents that distinguished them from their French equivalents. They lacked sensitivity to people's sufferings. It was a lack that was particularly useful in their unpleasant trade.

Hartmann swung round smartly and marched out as if he were on parade, leaving the admiral to his own thoughts. On the one hand he was confident in the knowledge that somehow or other he was on to something big. On the other he was a little worried. He didn't quite know why. Mercier wasn't really an imaginative man, but he was sensitive to atmosphere. This day he felt that something strange was happening here in Algeria which might well escape his control: something that might even shatter his own plans for the future.

100

He grunted and watched as, outside, the warder who had beaten the Jew with the dyed-black ritual locks fetched a bucket of sea water and flung it over his victim, out cold on the cobbles. The Jew came to, coughing and spluttering, and was pushed into line by other deportees.

Suddenly the Jew, his head still spurting blood from the guard's beating, looked up at Mercier standing there watching, as if he had known the Frenchman had been there all the time, and had known, too, that the latter had somehow been responsible for his cruel treatment. And there was a look of such unmitigated hatred in the Jew's dark eyes that Mercier reeled back, as if he had been struck an actual physical blow. 'No . . .' he began, he knew not why.

But it was too late for an explanation, if that was what Mercier had intended. The head guard, mounted on his horse, had blown a shrill blast on his whistle and the dreary bunch had already begun to move, their home-made kitbags slung over their weary shoulders. Mercier dabbed the sudden sweat from his brow with a hand that had started to tremble for reasons he could not fathom.

Three storeys below in the fortress's deepest cell, Hartmann had already ordered the prisoner to strip and had made a startling discovery almost at once. Below the camouflage smock, he had come across a strange uniform. It was a naval one all right, he'd known that at once. But it was unlike that of the Italian, French and German sailors who frequented Algiers in this year of 1942.

Now he paused and stared at the prisoner, puzzled about what to do next. How would he find out what kind of navy the battered captive belonged? Was he even a member of some navy? Perhaps he might be a merchant seaman? The jail was full of them, from all over the world – yellow, black, red – they were all present – deserters, men who had jumped ship, those who had been in punch-ups in the brothels, bars and cheap hotels their like frequented. When the prisoners were let out of their crowded cells that stank of sweat, sex and human misery for their daily hour of exercise, it was 'like the frigging Tower of frigging Babel', as he explained it to his cronies. 'Every frigging lingo under the sun.'

'Macaroni?' he tried. 'You Italian Macaroni?'

Smythe looked at the big crop-haired German in puzzlement. What was the bugger getting at it?

Hartmann tried again. 'Russki . . . *Govorit po russki?*'

That question in broken Russian exhausted Hartmann's knowledge of foreign languages. He knew German and broken French and that was about it, so how did he interrogate a prisoner when he could not make him understand the questions, and nor could he understand the man's answers? 'Heaven, arse and cloudburst!' he exploded in German, his face brick-red with frustration. What in three devils' name was he going to do?

Suddenly he had it. 'One Ball!' he exclaimed aloud, face suddenly gleaming with new hope. 'One Ball'll know.'

Five minutes later a puzzled Smythe, stretched out on his concrete slab, for he still felt weak from the night before, heard the heavy tread of the German returning, accompanied by the lighter tread of someone else. The cell door was flung open with a rusty squeak of hinges that had not been oiled these many years, to reveal a wisp of a man overshadowed by the huge ex-sergeant-major.

He could have been almost fifty, terribly skinny, so that his trusty uniform hung off him, as if it had been meant for a man twice his size, his sparse hair combed crosswise across his balding head and a knowing look in his sharp eyes. But it was none of these features which caught Smythe's gaze. It was the anchor tattooed on his right wrist where he had rolled up his too-long pyjama jacket.

Smythe caught his breath as he deciphered the writing that encircled the tattoo in a kind of an ornamental wreath. It read, *England Expects*. It was Nelson's old motto. Did it mean the little man with the sharp eyes was an Englishman, and more importantly a member of the Senior Service? Suddenly he felt new hope surge through his battered body. Perhaps he was going to get out of this damned mess after all?

Hartmann did not notice any of this; he was too eager to get on with his interrogation and find out what language the prisoner spoke. For the whore he was going to use to humiliate the prisoner was already on her way from the port's medical officer, where she had been examined to obtain her monthly certificate that stated she was free of VD. If he planned it right and got the cross-examination over with by the time Mercier wanted him, he might get a free bit of dancing the mattress polka from her; and he just fancied making the two-backed beast this afternoon. '*Bon!*' He turned to the little man with the sharp eyes. 'Find out who the prisoner is, One Ball. I'm in a hurry.'

The little man touched his hand to his balding head in mock salute, saying, 'Anything you wish, General . . .'

Book Three
Diplomat Among the Warriors

'Politics are almost as exciting as war, and quite as dangerous. In war you can only be killed once, but in politics many times.'

Winston Churchill

One

'Swell kid,' Clark exclaimed, as he waited for the seaplane to land which would fly him to Gibraltar so that he'd arrive there at least twenty-four hours before the *Seraph*. 'It took some guts to keep the Frogs at bay, while we escaped. Without orders too. I am certain that I can convince my boss, General Eisenhower, to award him the DSC for his outstanding courage.' He beamed at Commander Jewell.

'Yessir,' the commander of the *Seraph* replied dutifully, but without enthusiasm. By now he had got the measure of Churchill's 'American Eagle' and did not particularly like what he had discovered. Jewell felt that Clark was too full of himself. He had repeated the story of how he had lost his pants over and over again to anybody on the submarine – even the cook – who was prepared to listen to him. But he hadn't mentioned the fact that his group of US staff officers had also lost the highly secret papers that Mast had given him, detailing the French defences around Algiers.

That morning too, Clark had sent a message to his 'boss', as he called General Eisenhower, stating 'All questions . . . settled satisfactorily . . . Anticipate that the bulk of the French Army and Air Force will offer little resistance . . . Initial resistance by French Navy and coastal defences . . . will fall off rapidly as our forces advance.' Jewell, who had encoded the message intended for Eisenhower's eyes only, wondered, if that was the case, why had the French police searched so intensely for the American team. They had tried three times to apprehend them, a lot for the usually easy-going French.

Then Clark had requested a seaplane to take him from the middle of the Mediterranean to Gibraltar, as he was in a great hurry to report to General Eisenhower; the submarine was too

107

slow for him. Somehow Jewell didn't think that this was the real reason for his great hurry. Somehow he believed Clark wanted to give his version of what had happened at that meeting with General Mast before Jewell's own report trickled up channels and reached the Supreme Commander. He concluded that General Clark wasn't going to let anyone or anything spoil his triumph: the general 'who had lost his pants and had helped to win the war' sort of thing.

But now the Catalina seaplane was coming in slowly from the north, skimming the mirror-like surface of the sea, and the deck crew were assembling to bid their illustrious passenger (minus his staff) good-bye, complete with the bosun's whistle and all the traditional ritual of the Royal Navy.

Jewell nodded to his second-in-command. The young officer snapped out an order. Next to the conning tower, Sambo and Ferguson, still worse for wear due to the various tots of rum they had managed to down illegally, using all the cunning of SBS officers, stamped their feet and prepared to come to attention and salute the departing general. Out of the side of his mouth, Sambo, no respecter even of generals, hissed, 'What do you make of him?'

Ferguson, the strict Ulster protestant, whispered back, 'Bullshit, all pure bullshit, Sambo.'

The bigger of the two SBS officers nodded his agreement and added, 'It's going to be a funny old war with these Yanks taking over, old friend. God knows what kind of messes they're going get us into.' The rest of his complaint was drowned by the rear of the Catalina's single engine as the pilot throttled back and the seaplane came to a stop parallel with the submarine's conning tower.

Clark reached out for the plane's wing. Behind, the *Seraph*'s second-in-command bellowed, 'Ship's company . . . ship's company – *ashun*!'

The ratings, in their clean white pullovers, came to the position of attention. At the conning tower, the two SBS officers raised their right hands to their woollen caps. On the wing of the seaplane, Clark turned round, returned their salute gravely and said, 'I will not make a speech.'

'Thank God for that,' Sambo muttered under his breath.

'Save to say this. This has been an outstanding example of Allied co-operation. We Americans and British have made a good start to winning this war. Thank you and God bless you all.' He saluted and then, turning to the waiting American pilot, whispered, 'Gimme a cup of good ole American coffee, for God's sake. That British tea tastes like horse piss.' And with that, Churchill's 'American Eagle' set off to report to Eisenhower and tell the story of his 'great North African adventure' to the waiting representatives of the US Press before anyone else did. As the plane rose and disappeared into the clouds, General Clark told himself that if that story didn't earn him a fourth general's star, he'd eat his own goddam hat!

An hour later, Clark and Eisenhower were striding urgently down the subterranean village built in the great rock of Gibraltar. To left and right, signposts indicated the way to the 'Monkey Cave's Convalescent Hospital', the 'Jolly Jack Tar Laundry' and the like. Pipes ran overhead in all directions. Rats scuttled to and fro outside the pools of light cast by the naked electric light bulbs. Ventilation fans clattered noisily, making it difficult to converse. Not that it stopped Clark as he recounted his adventures, even forgetting to use the duck-boards which bridged the puddles in his eagerness, going up to his ankles more than once in mud.

Eisenhower, glad to see his old friend from West Point days back in one piece, listened attentively. But it was obvious he was worried and that his mind was elsewhere; and he was chain-smoking again, finishing one Camel after another, lighting a fresh one from the previous butt as soon as it appeared to be going out.

'In here, Wayne,' he said finally as they came to a stop, just as Clark was explaining, 'Out there, Ike, you'll see guys walking hand in hand. It doesn't mean they're queer. It's just their custom.'

Ike nodded briskly and said, 'I'll see the public relations boys spread the word among the troops.' And then, 'Here's my humble home.' With a wave of his hand he indicated the tight office, a small box walled with opaque glass. 'Take the weight off your legs and let's get down to cases.'

He lit another cigarette and rang for coffee. While he waited, he started immediately into the Torch situation. ''Kay, you say this General Mast guy is going to come through. Once we land, he'll order his troops not to oppose us.'

Clark nodded.

'Fine. But of course Mast doesn't know *when* we are going to land. As you've spelled it out, he thinks we're not landing for months yet.'

'Well, I could tell him little else . . .'

'Don't worry, Wayne, you did exactly as you were ordered to do,' Eisenhower cut him off sharply. The two generals might well be good friends, but Eisenhower knew Clark's weakness, especially his almost pathological desire not to be proven wrong. 'So it could be our invasion will take him by surprise and for various reasons he might not be in a position to control the activities of his troops. So this is what we're going to do.'

Clark realized that Eisenhower was in charge and he'd better keep his mouth shut for the time being; after all, it would be Ike who would put him in for that fourth general's star in due course.

Eisenhower answered his own question. 'We ought to be in a position to make an effective landing even if General Mast can't support us totally. Now, according to the studies we have made, the key to the defences of Algiers is this fort-cum-prison – according to Intelligence and what I've seen of the Mast documents you brought with you, Wayne. At the moment the fort is to be assaulted by Ryder's Thirty-Fourth Infantry Division. It's a good outfit and it has trained hard in Ireland, as you know. But the Thirty-Fourth has never seen action before.' Eisenhower lowered his gaze for a moment. Clark knew why. In all his years in the US Army, Eisenhower had never been under fire either. 'So I want a battle-hardened outfit to go in with Ryder's men just in case real fighting develops between us and the French.'

Clark looked puzzled. 'But where are you going to find that kind of outfit in the US Army, Ike? It's too late to draw in some outfit fighting the Nips in the Pacific, if there is one available.'

'It's not going to be an American unit, Wayne,' Eisenhower answered a little unhappily. 'It's going to be a limey one.'

110

'Limey! Hellfire, Ike, that'll set the cat among the pigeons if the French find out. They are strictly one-hundred per cent anti-British, whether Mr Churchill likes it or not.'

'He understands, Wayne. In fact I discussed the matter with the PM just before I left London. He's offered a British commando for the op.'

'But once the French see them—'

Again Eisenhower cut his old comrade off with a quick, 'What the French will see is an American outfit. The commando is going to dress in US uniform and use our weapons. Let's hope that Mast's men will take them at face value.'

'And if they don't, Ike?'

Eisenhower gave Clark a sombre look. 'Then the Britishers will have to fight for it. Let's face it, Wayne, we can't come ashore shouting, "Here we are again, Lafayette for the second time" sort of thing and then start firing on the Frogs. Let the Britishers take the blame if it comes to that.'

'That's kinda cynical, Ike,' Clark opined carefully.

'Agreed, Wayne. But the world in which we're living is a cynical one. We're not only playing the French along, we're doing the same with Churchill and his people. You don't know Washington like I do. Once this French North African business is cleared up and we have victory, do you think that FDR is going to let the British and the French keep their empires in that part of the world?' Eisenhower shook his head. 'Not a chance. Special relationship or not, the British and later the French are going to be made by us to give up their colonial empires. One other thing,' Eisenhower flushed now, his hand shaking with agitation as he puffed at his Camel, warmed to his subject. 'I'm going to take no chances with your General Mast. You're going to signal him, Wayne, that we are coming and that hell and high water and the whole of his North African army can't stop us, and that if he uses the information about our operations that we've already entrusted to him to our disadvantage, we'll hang him higher than a kite when we get ashore.' Eisenhower paused from so much talk, chest heaving, while Clark stared at him aghast, realizing just how much his old comrade had changed from the easy-going Ike with ready ear-to-ear smile since he had become Allied Supreme Commander.

For what seemed an age, there was a heavy silence in the little underground office, broken only by the wheezing and gasping of the heating system, until Eisenhower broke it with, 'This came to me yesterday from your wife. Your new fame seems to have preceded you, Wayne. Maurine has got it all there for you.' He watched in an almost paternalistic manner as Clark opened the buff War Department envelope and pulled out the contents.

Clark whistled softly as he read the first item. 'Gee,' he exclaimed, 'Louella Parsons, the gossip columnist, says that I'm "America's dream hero".' He turned to the next cutting from his wife. 'The *Boston Globe* says here, that I've got a permanent place in the list of American heroes . . . Nathan Hale the first such American . . . I'm the latest.'

'Attaboy,' Eisenhower said without enthusiasm. He'd already planned that if things went wrong in North Africa, Clark was going to be the fall guy. It had taken him too long to get this far in his military career.

He was not going to lose everything because Clark might have screwed up. 'And what does your wife say?'

Clark fumbled with the last piece. It was a telegram from Western Union. He read it out loud. 'It's from the Amalgamated Clothing Workers of the United States. They state that "He(I) lost his trousers honorably. He is a living example of the fact that a great hero need not lose his dignity thereby . . . The most skilled pants makers in the world will be honored to make and present as many pairs of trousers as he may need in bringing the war to the enemy."'

Eisenhower laughed. 'Well, Wayne, you'll never be ragged-assed again, whatever happens to your pension. But seriously, Wayne, that's an example of how we Americans are going to win this war. Public opinion. Good public opinion. Get the ordinary Joe Doe on your side back home and victory is just round the corner . . . Yessir, public opinion is how we Americans are going to win the war . . .'

Two

Big, brutal face contorted with disgust, Hartmann slammed his fist into Smythe's face for the last time. As before, the young officer crashed into the cell wall, blood spurting afresh from his broken nose. His skinny body afire with pain, it seemed to him at that moment that the big German bully had broken virtually every bone in his body.

Hartmann spat on his knuckles. He was frustrated. Again he had gotten nothing out of the damned Tommy officer and he didn't like that one bit. The man who boasted to his cronies in the Bar de la Legion that he could make a mummy talk, prided himself that he'd break his victims in the end, wasn't used to prisoners like this. The Tommy was a skinny little piss pansy, but he was like a hunk of steel wire. He moaned and groaned like the rest did. But he didn't frigging well talk. He'd have to see the admiral about him, and he knew it wouldn't be a pleasant experience. When the admiral wanted something, he wanted it quick.

He aimed an idle kick at the man on the floor's ribs. The Englishman grunted and coughed up some more blood. Otherwise he didn't seem to feel the blow. Hartmann told himself the tea-drinking bastard didn't have any nerves. 'All right,' he said to the trustee who had acted as his interpreter. 'Get him cleaned up the best you can. We might have to take him up to the Admiral. And you know Mercier. He doesn't like to come in contact with you nasty filthy prisoners.'

Again the little English trustee touched his fingers to his balding head in mock salute. '*Oui, mon General,*' he said.

Hartmann gave him a hard look. 'And none of your lip, you frigging runt. Or you'll get the back o' my hand in zero, comma, nuthin' seconds.'

113

The little English trustee didn't react. If he were afraid, he didn't show it. Instead, as he bent over a semi-conscious Smythe, he whispered, 'And you can stick that where the sun doesn't shine, Matey.'

He waited till Hartmann had slammed the cell door behind him before pulling the little flask of cheap rum from beneath his dirty striped tunic. Almost gently he held the little flask to Smythe's cracked, blood-scummed lips. 'Here you are, sir. Get a dose of Nelson's blood behind yer collar stud.'

The 'Nelson's Blood' remark caused Smythe to open his eyes, though he would have dearly loved to lapse into unconsciousness and blot all this pain and misery out for a while. Dimly, through his puffed-up eyes, he caught a wavering glimpse of the trustee holding the flask up for him. He took a sip like a willing baby suckling its mother's breast. Next moment he started to cough furiously while the trustee fussed and tut-tutted.

Finally the coughing was over and now Smythe could feel the fiery spirit coursing through his battered body, giving him new hope and interest in his surroundings, in particular in the little trustee with his tattoo that indicated he had once served in the Royal Navy. But what was he doing here . . . and working for the big German and his master the admiral, who was obviously a German tool as well?

The trustee seemed to read his thoughts. For, as he tried to dab the blood from Smythe, wetting his dirty cloth by spitting on it as he did so, he whispered, keeping his eyes on the cell door, 'Call me Jem, sir. I was a three-striper on the old *Barham* when she was torpedoed in the Med back in '40. Regular, sir,' he added as if it were important, 'not one of yer frigging HO* nancy boys.'

'But how did you land up in this hellhole?' Smythe asked weakly as Jem fed him another sip of the cheap rum.

'A long story. But let's say I thought I'd done my bit for the Old Country, and then I hit a froggie officer who was getting too familiar with the lady –' he lowered his voice, as

Hostilities Only, men who had been called up to the Navy for the duration of the war.

114

if he were approaching a very delicate subject – 'who was looking after me.'

'You mean you were living with a woman here in French Algeria?'

'Yes, something like that. Doing no bugger no harm. Just getting along with a few black-market deals in the Kasbah, when it all went askew and I landed here. Though it weren't too bad for me. I had a lot of friends and associates in here, especially the towelheads. So I really wasn't wanting for much. Even manage to get my leg over now and again when the guards are in a generous mood.' He made the continental gesture of counting bank notes with his dirty thumb and forefinger.

If he had been capable of doing so, Smythe would have laughed at the little man. He was a typical old sweat, always on the lookout for the main chance and always, so it seemed, landing on his two feet, come what may. Now, however, as weak and hurting as he was, he realized that Jem was the only hope he possessed. Obviously the ex-three-striper didn't particularly dislike his life inside the fort-cum-prison. He had his three squares, and occasionally, as he put it, he could 'manage to get his leg over', and, as trustee, he seemed to have the run of the place; he even got on with the German, Hartmann. Would he risk all that for his, Smythe's, sake? At Jem's age security and peace of mind meant a lot.

Smythe licked the rest of the bloody scum from his lips, feeling as he did so that most of his front teeth were loose from Hartmann's cruel beating. 'Jem.'

'Sir?'

'I don't know what your position on the war is . . .'

Jem smiled, revealing that his front teeth were not just loose, but non-existent; they had vanished long ago. 'The war, sir?' he echoed, suddenly thoughtful. 'A lot o' folk think we've lost it. But now the Yanks are in –' he shrugged his skinny shoulders – 'perhaps we might win it. I hope so for the sake of the old country. But for me, well sir, to be honest, I've opted out.'

'Really?'

'Well, I think I've done my bit. You know, I was at Jutland in '16 on the old *Iron Duke*. I should have got out the Royal

115

after that. But, bloody fool me, I stayed on. Went through all the troubles in the '20s when the big shots in London cut our pay – lost my first missus after that. Then this new lot. Second missus killed in the bombing of Pompey. Then the *Barham* . . .' His voice trailed away to nothing, as if he felt he'd said enough, or perhaps didn't know how to explain any further to this young officer, who was still wet behind the ears and had no concept of the life of a sailor on the lower deck.

'But you're still British, Jem,' Smythe said softly, breaking the silence.

Jem nodded cautiously. 'I am that, sir . . . and I suppose I'm still proud of it.'

'Well, Jem, would you like to see big bullies like Hartmann running the world, or that boss of his, the French Admiral?'

Jem tugged the end of his permanently red nose. 'Well, there's not much I can do about that, sir. I'm just a lower-deck rating who's been beached these couple of years or more.' His voice rose. 'Not that I'm scared of Hartmann. The bigger they are, the harder they fall. As my dear old mum used to say, there's many a big tatie that's rotten.'

Smythe tried to smile at the expression. It didn't work. It was much too painful to do so. 'We're all nobodies really, Jem,' he said, slightly amazed at himself as he spoke. For up to now he had never really philosophized on the meaning of the war. 'But together we're somebody.' Inside his brain a little voice sneered, *Christ Almighty, you sound like one of those bloody propaganda films, written by some left-wing parlour pink who'd run a ruddy mile if he ever saw a live Jerry soldier.* 'And we can do something. You see, Jem, I can't tell you much, but I can say this. I've get to get out of this place before I crack and tell that Jerry bully the little bit I know. If I do crack and blab . . .' He didn't finish his sentence. Instead he held up his hands in a gesture of near despair.

The old sailor swallowed hard. 'It's a bit hard, sir. I mean to say, where do I go from here, which I would have to do if I helped you? I'd have to do a bunk as well. The Navy wouldn't have me back. In fact they'd have me on the rattle straight off and I'd more than likely end up in the glasshouse.'

Smythe could see he was wavering. At the same time he

could understand Jem's point of view. What would happen to the old sailor if he managed to get him out of this prison? If the French didn't get him and he made it to some British territory, he would more than likely be court-martialled as a deserter, and Smythe, new boy to the Navy as he was, knew what the possible penalty for desertion in the face of the enemy might be. *Death by hanging!*

'I understand your position, Jem,' he said hurriedly. 'I don't want to force you . . .' He stopped. He could see the old sailor wasn't really listening. His wrinkled old face was contorted as if he were deep in thought. Smythe waited. Finally Jem said, 'All right, sir. If I can find a way out, you're on.'

Smythe's battered face lit up. 'God bless you, Jem,' he exclaimed.

'I hope he does, sir. I'll need all the help I can get for this one. Mostly the likes of us usually get shit on from above.' And with these words of wisdom he went to the door, rattled it for the guard, shouting in his terrible French, 'Come on, you wog arse with ears, *ouvrez, vite . . .*' Then he was gone, leaving Smythe feeling a new sense of hope.

Three floors above where the prisoner lay on the concrete slab, wanting urgently to urinate, but knowing that it was going to hurt like hell to pass water after the pounding Hartmann had given his kidneys, Admiral Mercier positioned himself under the whirling fan to enjoy the artificial breeze. For it was one of those sultry days in autumn in Algiers which heralded a storm to come. Over on the sea, dark clouds were rolling in landwards. Here and there lightning zig-zagged silently across them. Below, in the palms that fringed the quayside, the camels and goats cropped the sparse grass fitfully, tossing their heads nervously, as if they already knew what was to come soon.

Mercier mopped his brow delicately with his snow-white handkerchief, while a waiting Hartmann wished he'd get on with it. He could just sink a litre of cold beer, even if it was that camel piss the local breweries made. 'Let's have a look at what we've already got,' Mercier said suddenly.

'Sir?'

'Hartmann, you're not in the German Army now. We don't

117

spring to attention – and so noisily – every time an officer farts,' Mercier chided him. Sometimes it did his soul good to reprimand these German-born legionnaires, just because they belonged to the nation which had beaten *la belle France*.

'Yessir . . . Sorry, sir.' Again Hartmann clicked his heels together as he had been taught to do years before in Berlin.

Mercier looked at the ceiling as if he were seeking solace from heaven. None came and he got on with it. '*One*, something strange went on at the Teissier house and it was not connected with smuggling, as the local police thought. *Two*, our people were involved subsequently in a firefight and these days it takes a daring local, even an Arab, to fire on the police. It is a dangerous thing to do. *Third*, we find this chap you've got below in the cells and he turns out to be a swine of an English naval officer. So we have a strange situation and from it we can conclude at the moment only this – due to your inability to get anything out of the man.' He looked severely at Hartmann.

'Sorry, sir. But my hands are tied. You have not allowed me to work him over—'

Mercier waved for him to shut up and Hartmann did so promptly. The last thing he wanted to do was to get on the wrong side of Admiral Mercier. 'Something happened in the Teissier house involving the British, who were prepared to fight, so it was important. The Americans were involved in some way or other, I've found out. The man that little dead runt was supposed to meet in the Algiers Cathedral was a certain Mister Robert Murphy, a Catholic *and* the American chargé d'affaires to our own government. A very important American indeed. So, I ask you, Hartmann, what is an American diplomat – who has been presented to Marshal Petain* himself and routinely dines with Admiral Darlan when he is in France – doing meeting British naval officers at that lonely cliff-top house – and engaging indirectly in shooting matches with our local police, eh?'

Hartmann looked blank. It was how Mercier expected him to look. After all, the man was all muscle and little brain.

*Head of the pro-German Vichy puppet French governmentt.

Indeed, Mercier knew he was merely bouncing his own ideas off the wooden-headed German sergeant-major.

'I shall tell you what it means,' Mercier continued slowly. 'It means that the Anglo-Americans, prompted as always by those cunning English swine, are up to something here in Africa. It might be to raise the Arabs against us. I doubt it, however. The English have trouble enough with their own colonies – especially in India, where the Japanese are about to invade and take the subcontinent away from them.' Mercier shook his head. 'No, it's something else, Hartmann. And I have an awful feeling we've got to find out what it is soon. So, Hartmann, get working on that Englishman. Tell that little runt who does your translating that we'll make life even easier if *he* can get something out of the prisoner.'

'*Jawohl, Herr Admiral!*' Again Hartmann stamped his foot down and Mercier suppressed a groan.

'In the meantime, I'll have a closer look at *Mister* Robert Murphy . . .'

Three

B ut Admiral Mercier was not the only one that evening who was preparing to approach the most senior American in Algiers. Despite his age and his stupid toothless unkempt appearance, Jem was nobody's fool. He had already guessed the young naval officer now eating his tin bowl of thin watery soup in the lower cells of the fortress-cum-prison had not arrived in French North Africa by himself. He had had support from others already in Algeria. And he had also guessed it couldn't only be dissident North African Frenchmen. Of course, there were enough hot-headed kids running about who maintained they were supporting de Gaulle. He had met some of them in the prison. But they could not keep a secret to save their lives – and besides, they had no power; they were simply students mouthing a lot of bullshit about democracy and freedom and that sort of crap.

Jem also wondered who among the higher-ranking French – the military and the *functionnaires* – might be involved. That lot, he knew, were more concerned with promotion and their pensions – the Frogs always did their nuts worrying about their frigging pensions – than the fact that the Jerries had given them a right pasting in '40 and that they were now at the beck and call of the squareheads. He concluded that if they were involved, they'd be keeping it very much to themselves. It was then, just as the bugler on the fort's ramparts was beginning to sound lights out for the prisoners, that he realized. It could be the Yanks, though there were only a handful of them in Algiers, flogging guns and planes and the like to the French Army. They were mostly drunken salesmen, out to make money and getting their greasy paws up Frog women's drawers. So it had to be someone else. But who?

It was half an hour later when Hartmann brought Anne-Marie from the brothel across the way, saying, 'Here you are. You've got half an hour. I've paid for you, you dirty little bugger.'

Jem whistled softly. 'But it ain't my turn for a bit of it for another three weeks, Sergeant-Major,' he protested mildly, eyeing the whore, whose melon-like breasts were threatening to burst out of her cheap artificial silk blouse at any moment.

'Don't worry, you little Tommy piss pansy,' Hartmann growled. 'You're gonna pay for it one way or another. Give me a hand with that English shit down there in the cells tonight and she's yours for an hour. And yer can't say I ain't being generous. There's good-quality meat loaf there, comrade, and plenty of it.' He gave Anne-Marie's plump bottom what he considered a playful pat with his big paw, which sent her stumbling to the wall. 'All right, get on with it . . . and use a Parisian –' he meant a contraceptive – 'I don't want to have to explain you getting a dose of the clap.' And with that he was gone, leaving the two of them alone, and Anne-Marie cursing under her breath, '*Sale boche*, slapping my rear. If he goes on like that I'll be taking my knife to him one day, and it won't be his frigging big ears I'll be slicing off, I can tell you.'

'Now don't talk like that, Anne-Marie,' Jem said soothingly, trying to evade her big heaving bosom with his wizened face, for she was a head taller than he was. 'He don't mean it. He can't help being a Boche.' He curved his hand around her waist and pressed her lovingly so that she calmed down immediately, saying, 'Now, you're different, Jem. You've got a heart o' gold.'

'And something else,' he whispered, pressing himself against her, 'Can't yer feel it? And it ain't me fountain pen I've got in my pocket neither.'

She giggled and pressed his balding head against that massive chest of hers so that he was gasping for air in a matter of seconds. But even as he was working himself up for the pleasure to come, Jem was already planning which Americans he'd approach. As he already knew, even as trustee prisoner they'd never let him leave the jail, but the big whore with her dyed blonde hair was another matter altogether . . .

*   *   *

121

Robert Murphy rubbed his eyes wearily. It had been another long day in the airless room – above him the ceiling fan seemed merely to shift the air around listlessly and not cool him. Not that he'd had much time to notice the fact until now. All day the French – pro-Gaullists, Vichy officials, military, and both Arabs and *pieds noirs* – had been out to make a deal with the new hope for everyone – the Americans. For the locals, whatever their political sympathies, all believed the rich Americans would now win the war. They had done so in France against the Germans in 1918, and they would do so again, perhaps not this year of 1942, but soon. And all his visitors wanted to be on the winning side.

Murphy sighed and wished he had been a soldier rather than a diplomat. Soldiers' lives were much simpler; pretty well cut and dried, black and white most of the time. A diplomat, on the other hand, had to deal with half-truths, sometimes downright lies. The strain was tremendous. Simply remembering the lies one had told to people required a lot of brain power.

General Mast was a case in point. He had lied to him that he'd have months to prepare for the American invasion of North Africa. Instead of that, it would be a matter of weeks before Eisenhower sent his troops ashore at Algiers and in the other two French African colonies. What would Mast do when he realized he had been tricked, or at least misled? Would he go back on his word not to defend the Algerian coastline? Or would he be in a position to help the American invaders when they landed much earlier than he had anticipated?

Murphy rose from his big, paper-littered desk and, walking across the room, looked at himself in the fly-blown mirror on the wall. He seemed to have aged in the last few days. There were deep black circles under his eyes, his cheeks appeared to be sunken and what looked like dandruff clung to his bowed shoulders.

'Holy Mary, Mother of God,' he moaned like his Irish grandmother might have done. 'Now I'm losing my goddam hair, too.'

It was then that the discreet quiet knock came at the door.

He forgot his worried mood. Hurriedly he crossed to the door and unlocked it. These days he always kept the door locked, even when he was inside the office. The place contained too many secrets and he didn't trust Admiral Mercier's spies and agents; they'd break into the place even though it meant infringing his neutral and diplomatic status.

It was Teddy, one of his twelve 'apostles', as he, the good Catholic, called them: those Americans in North Africa who would help him to make the landings successful when the day of the invasion came. When they received the signal from London, thanks to the BBC – *''Allo, Robert . . . Franklin arrive'* – Teddy and the other 'apostles' would supervise the various French resistance groups who would take over the radio stations, centres of transport, police stations and the like. In addition, they would place little groups of pro-de Gaulle young men, armed, around the various headquarters of Mast's 19th Corps to ensure the soldiers didn't go back on their word to offer no resistance to the invaders. In essence, he and his apostles would attempt to ensure that the Americans would be able to take over Algiers, the capital, without a shot being fired.

Hastily the two of them shook hands. Murphy locked the door once more and asked the much younger American, 'What brings you here this late, Teddy? I thought you'd be out carousing again – that wine, women and song of yours . . .'

Teddy, very much the Phillips Academy/Harvard smoothie that he was, gave Murphy that splendid gleaming white-toothed smile of his and said, 'Now, you know me, Mr Murphy.' His smile broadened. 'Well, forget the song at least.' His smile vanished. 'Something's turned up which you might like to look into. In fact, I feel you *should* look into it.'

'Trouble?'

'Perhaps.'

'In what form, Teddy?'

'A woman in the first place – a woman of the streets,' Teddy added carefully, knowing that the 'chief' was pretty moral. His idea of a night out was a meal in a fancy restaurant with not too much juice.

'You mean a whore, Teddy?'

'Yes, I do, and she won't tell me why in particular she wants to see you.' He stuck his neck out and added with a cheeky grin, 'You haven't done anything naughty, have you?'

'Teddy, I do naughty things every day, but not the kind you have in mind. All right then, let's wheel in this – er – lady of the night of yours.'

A few moments later, Murphy's Arab servant, a look of disapproval on his dark, hook-nosed face, ushered in Anne-Marie, all clacking high heels and bouncing breasts. The Arab's frown increased as he took in the whore's ample figure, of which she was showing too much. If his master had asked for a boy in a discreet manner, he would have approved, but he had only disgust for this whore.

Murphy didn't notice. He said in his good French, 'M'selle, what can I do for you? What brings you here at this time of the night?'

Normally Anne-Marie wasn't impressed by men. She had spent nearly twenty years on her back satisfying their sexual needs, which had come in all shapes and sizes. For her, a man with his trousers down, panting like a rabid dog, was not an impressive sight. But this balding American sat behind his big desk with the eagle of his country above his head and flanked by furled flags was somehow or other different – he looked so stern, too, and for a moment she was lost for words.

Again Murphy repeated his questions while Teddy eyed her up and down in his professional way, telling himself she'd be all right for a quick tumble on the mattress – she looked as if she knew every perversion under the sun. But she might be dangerous. A guy might just come away from her bed with a painful souvenir. But before the American had time to consider the possibility any further, Anne Marie said with a *pieds-noirs* accent, 'A friend has suggested that you may help us, M'sieu. It is urgent.'

'A friend?' Murphy mused, in no way agitated at her words. But then he was the consumate diplomat who had been long accustomed never to show surprise. 'Who? What kind of friend is this, M'selle?'

Swiftly, her magnificent chest heaving with the effort, she told Murphy about Jem and the prisoner. *'Un anglais, M'sieu . . . Un officier.'*

124

At the mention of the English naval officer, Murphy showed some emotion for the first time. He held up his hand, as if he were some New York Irish-American cop holding up the traffic. 'An English officer, you said?'

'Yessir.'

'Tell me more, please,' Murphy said, his heart racing wildly. Clark had yet to signal him that they had lost one of the boat party that crazy night at Teissier's place. Was this a provocation by the Vichy people? If it wasn't and Mercier's people had gotten hold of one of the landing party, they'd soon squeeze the truth out of him and then all hell would be let loose. Now he had to know if the whore was telling the truth.

Anne-Marie didn't need any urging. She could see the American was interested and, by the looks of him and his office, he was rich. There'd be money in this one for her, if she played her cards right, as Jem had promised her there would be. She went on to explain further, while Murphy's subtle brain was already working out a plan just in case she was telling the truth.

'So, this Jem of yours is prepared to take the risk of breaking out with the English officer, if we are ready to pay him and get him out of Algeria?'

Anne-Marie answered in the affirmative, already wondering what she should ask for her assistance. For she guessed she'd have to take a dive in the Kasbah* if she helped. Then the *flics* would be looking for anyone who'd had dealings with the trustee Jem in the last forty-eight hours or so; and she had definitely had several dealings with him, the dirty little bugger. He'd gone at it like a fiddler's elbow.

Murphy frowned as he noted the smile on the whore's face. This was a terrible situation; nobody should be smiling now. He spoke. 'Would you be willing to help us?'

She nodded, making the gesture of counting notes with her beringed right hand as she did so. 'For a consideration, sir.'

'The consideration will be forthcoming,' he assured her swiftly. He turned to Teddy and said in rapid English, which

*The native quarter in Algiers, walled and difficult for the French authorities to enter.

125

he hoped the harlot didn't understand, 'Would you be willing to take over this bloody business? Get in contact with her Jem, arrange a deal and rally with this officer in the Kasbah?'

'Of course, Chief. I'd be delighted to do so. It'll be a great adventure to tell my grandkids.' He smiled winningly.

Murphy's flat Irish face remained solemn. 'If you live long enough to have 'em . . . All right, this is the deal . . .'

Outside, Mercier's agent had seen enough. Swiftly he walked to the phone box and dialed the number the admiral had given him. 'Sir,' he said rapidly, keeping his gaze fixed on the door of the consulate, where a big American car with diplomatic plates had now drawn up, its lights dimmed. 'There's something going on. They've got the prison whore . . .'

Four

'*Bollocks!*' Jem grunted, then he whispered, 'Please excuse my French, sir. I'm not very couth, sir.'

In spite of the soreness of his jaw, where half an hour before a frustrated and angry Hartmann had planted a last punch with a fist like a steam shovel, Smythe forced a grin. 'Don't worry, Jem,' he whispered back. 'I've heard worse.'

The two of them were crouched in a kind of tunnel between the inner and outer wall of the old fortress-cum-prison. Once, according to Jem, it had been used by the native jailers to transport prisoners secretly from the cellars to the flat roof, where, as Jem had put it in his own charming way, 'They kicked the poor sods up the Khyber and sent them into the Med for a one-way trip.' Now they were going to use it for their own exit.

Ever since an angry Hartmann had departed from the latest bout of interrogation, muttering about the '*Englische Schweinehund*' who didn't have sense enough to talk now before he was condemned to start 'looking at the potatoes from below the ground', things had happened fast to Horatio Smythe. Jem had waited till the sound of Hartmann's boots had vanished down the corridor before he had declared in a hushed whisper, 'We're gonna make a run for it, sir.'

He had patted the blood from his face and nose and had said thickly through his damaged organ, 'Make a run for it?'

'Yessir. Before that square-headed bugger made his appearance, Anne-Marie's kid brother contacted me. He has no trouble with the screws. He's a bum boy, sir, yer see. He gives 'em a little bit o' the other and they let him in to see me. Anne-Marie's family's a rum lot, you see.'

Smythe had not even dared to think just how rum they were. Instead he had said. 'He's going to help us, Jem?'

'That he is, sir. If we can get on the roof, he and the people Anne-Marie went to see will help us.'

'It's not some sort of a trap?' he had queried hastily.

'No sir. I'm sure of that. These people have fixed Anne-Marie up in the Kasbah, so the kid brother said, and that costs coin of the realm. Besides, offer that tart money and she's your frigging friend for life.'

Smythe had asked no further questions. He knew he had to rely on the little deserter from the Royal Navy. He had no other choice. He was sure he couldn't stand another beating from Hartmann, who he guessed would employ more drastic methods to get him to talk on the morrow. He had gone along with Jem, who picked two locks inside of five minutes flat, and then got them to the inner wall. Here Jem had groped in the grey darkness, pausing every now and again to listen for any change in the steady, heavy-booted pace of the guards patrolling the outer wall.

Finally Jem had found the opening and had rolled back the concealed door, which had surprised Smythe, for it did not give off the slightest squeak. 'Used the fish oil from the evening tin of sardines, sir,' Jem had explained hastily. 'Come on, sir. We can't just stand here, sir, like a spare prick at a wedding.'

Smythe had followed the advice, wrinkling his nose at the stink of stale, fetid air from the inside the wall and the steps leading upwards towards the roof. But before they proceeded to climb them, Jem insisted on wrapping their shoes in the dirty rags he had brought with him specifically for this purpose, adding, 'Not a word now, sir . . . Remember the screws are just on the other side of that wall. They don't know about this staircase but they soon will if yer give even a delicate little fart—'

'Which I'm not about to do,' Smythe interrupted him. 'Lead on, Macduff.'

Jem led on.

Time seemed leaden as the two of them crept silently up the ancient stairs which had once led to sudden death for the white victims of the Barbary pirates who had maintained a reign of terror along this coast for hundreds of years till the

US Marines had finally broken their power in the early nineteenth century. Now and again the two disparate Englishmen stopped dead, their hearts beating furiously, alarmed by a sudden strange noise. But it was merely the clawed scamper of the rats which they had disturbed, despite their silence, hurrying back into their holes, which lined the staircase.

But finally the stale air started to give way to fresher, and then a slight breeze, salty and cooler, which indicated they were approaching the roof that overlooked the bay below. They pressed on faster, knowing that Smythe's absence could be discovered at any moment and that then all hell would be let loose.

Moments later they bumped into what appeared to be a blank wall. But Jem knew differently. 'We're here,' he hissed. 'Don't do nuthin' till I find the way out . . . Don't think they'll have a guard up here. But yer never know with the Frogs. Tricky, treacherous bastards.'

Smythe didn't answer. He couldn't. He was too worked up and feared that the quiver in his voice might well tell the other man just how scared he was. So he kept his mouth shut and waited till Jem spoke again to announce, 'Got it. Now, ready, sir. I'm gonna open up. Keep yer eyes peeled, please.'

'Like the proverbial tinned tomato, Jem,' was about all that Smythe could manage. He waited expectantly.

A creak. This time the concealed door wasn't oiled. To a startled Smythe it seemed that the whole of Algiers must have heard the noise. He tensed yet again. Nothing happened. Gingerly Jem began to open the door to the flat roof wider. Smythe could feel the cold sea air now coming in from straight across the bay. He took a deep breath. The air felt good after the stale muggy atmosphere of the cells below. Jem whispered, 'All clear, sir. Let's be having you. But keep low. We don't want to be spotted by the guards below. Those sods fire first and ask questions afterwards. All right, let's go.' His voice died away as he slipped on to the roof, which fortunately was dark, untouched by the silver light of the sickle moon.

A moment later Smythe followed the skinny old three-striper, to crouch below the level of the narrow parapet, waiting for what was to happen next. Jem, careful as he was, didn't waste time. He placed his two fingers between his blackened stumps of front teeth and whistled softly. Smythe crouched next to him, turned his head into the wind so that he could hear better. For what seemed an age, nothing happened. Then suddenly, startlingly, there was the soft honk of an old rubber car horn. Once . . . twice . . . three times. Jem pressed his arm hard. 'Don't say nowt. It's the signal all right. But we're not in the clear yet, sir.'

Smythe nodded his understanding. He wasn't afraid now; he had the utmost confidence in Jem's ability to get them out of the hellhole of a prison. All the same, his nerves were on edge. For he knew – instinctively – a great deal hung on his ability to escape and avoid being questioned again. For if he were taken prisoner once more and interrogated, he'd break, and God only knew what the enemy would make of his confession.

A soft whistle. Jem pressed his arm harder, so that it hurt. 'It's them. Hope you learned to climb the rigging at Dartmouth,' he added obscurely. Smythe frowned, puzzled. He wondered what Jem meant. Next moment he found out. There was an alarming loud clank. 'What the Christ . . . ?' he began as the metal hooks of a rope ladder hit the low parapet.

'It's them,' Jem cut him off swiftly.

As the unknowns below tugged harder to check if the hooks had caught hold properly, Jem seized Smythe's hand like a doting mother might do that of some spoiled child. 'Come on . . . We're on.'

Crouched low, they doubled to the hooks and now Smythe realized what Jem had meant about climbing the rigging at Dartmouth College. Fortunately he had, and he'd enjoyed doing so after he had overcome his first fears. Jem gave the hooks a hefty tug. 'Right.' He turned to Smythe. 'You first, sir. Don't panic if anything goes wrong. Just freeze for a moment. Once yer down, do as they say. No messing about.'

As tense as he was, Smythe could not but admire the deserter's air of command. 'Christ, Jem, how you stayed on the lower deck as an ordinary matelot for so long, I'll never know. You ought to have been running the ship.'

'Man o' the people, sir,' Jem declared stoutly. 'Off you go.'

Instantly Smythe swung his right leg over the parapet and on to the first rung of the rope ladder, then shifting to the right side so that the ladder didn't sway too much. Next moment he was shinning down it like a monkey, his aches and pains forgotten at once.

'Over here,' a voice hissed. The accent was American and he guessed he might be dealing with General Clark's people. But he had no time to consider the matter. The American whispered. 'Over there in the shadows. You'll see the automobile.' The American pushed him gently and hissed, 'Here comes your buddy. Move it, Lieutenant.'

Smythe 'moved it', aware of the faint noise that Jem was making as he came swinging down the rope ladder like some barefoot rating in training who was half his age. 'In here, M'sieu,' the voice ordered. The English was not quite right, and Smythe guessed the American had a local French helper. The rear door of the car opened and he swung himself in.

In that same instant an angry voice, somewhere close by, yelled, '*Qui est là? Que tu fait?*'

Smythe froze inside the car. On the ladder, still halfway down the sheer white wall of the fort, Jem did the same.

Again the guard repeated the challenge. There was the sound of heavy boots running across the *pavé* outside the place. A harsh official voice cried, '*Allez . . . vite . . . lumière!*' Behind the wheel the Frenchman cursed.

A searchlight clicked on. Smythe groaned aloud as the bright white light stabbed the velvet darkness and another voice yelled, '*Il est là, mon captaine!*' The light rose up the wall. Smythe could imagine what Jem was feeling at that moment. Should he jump? Should he hang on in the hope the light wouldn't detect him? 'Hell's bells,' he cursed aloud. 'If I only had a pistol . . .'

Too late. A voice ordered, '*Tirez!*'

There was the sudden frenetic chatter of a machine pistol, firing a full burst. Jem screamed piteously as his lower body was sawn in half. Next moment he flung up his arms wildly, losing his grip on the ladder and falling crazily to the cobbles. He slammed into them with a sickening thud. Smythe bit his bottom lip, praying silently that the poor little deserter would get up. But that wasn't to be. A sound of heavy boots crossing the *pavé*. A voice commanded, *'Tu, caporal!'*

'Qui, mon Capitaine?'

The answer came in German, *'Mach das Schwein kalt!'*

Smythe didn't understand German, but the officer's tone told him all he needed to know. They were going to kill his new friend and helper in cold blood. *'No!'* he screeched.

To no avail. In the same instant there came the single dry crack of a rifle being fired, and the unknown Frenchman started up the car, with the American jumping in, crying urgently, 'For Chrissakes, let's get the hell outa here!' Jem gave one last pitiful scream as the rifle bullet shattered the back of his head and he was dead. A moment later they were roaring away, heading for the safety of the Kasbah, red flashes of flame slashing the darkness behind them . . .

Book Four

Battle

'An appeaser is one who feeds a crocodile hoping it will eat him last.'

Winston Churchill

One

Carefully the elderly captain in the RAMC finished painting around his genitals with the white paste, saying, 'Don't worry. It isn't plaster of Paris, lieutenant. But it will harden somewhat. No problem really. We'll get it off easily enough tomorrow.'

'Yes,' Smythe said apathetically. A month or so before, he would have been terribly embarrassed at sitting there totally naked on the stool in the chilly cavern below the rock, having his body painted this way. But not now. He had been through too much since his capture.

'It's standard operating procedure with you chaps who have escaped from the Boche to go on the run. We cover you like this, let the stuff harden and then when we peel it off hours later. All the ticks and other dangerous things that your skin might have picked up from rough living will come away with it. Simple, what?' He smiled and applied one last bit of white goo to beneath Smythe's left testicle with a professional flourish, to step back then, head cocked to one side in order to admire his workmanship.

'Thanks, doctor,' Smythe said without any enthusiasm.

'Don't worry,' the elderly captain said. 'The Yanks have sent you down some beer and a packet of mail from the UK for you to read.' He took off his surgical gloves and looked at his hands thoughtfully before saying, 'You know, we sawbones should wash our hands more. God knows what we pass on to our patients. But this day I'll wash mine carefully enough, I can assure you.'

Without any interest, Smythe rose to the bait and asked, 'Why?'

'Pox. Bunch of bloody Yank sailors managed to get across

135

the Spanish border to the whorehouses in La Linea. Naturally they're poxed up to the eyeballs now. I'm off to give 'em the catheter up their waterworks. The umbrella, the lads call it. It certainly makes their eyes water when you open the thing out inside them and clean them out. Piss in seven different directions afterwards.' He tightened the straps of his medical haversack, complete with red cross. 'Serves 'em right. Those Yanks really do think they can get away with anything. Well, good luck, if you're going in with the rest down there in the harbour.'

He gave Smythe a brief professional smile and Smythe half raised his white-painted arm, as if in salute, but then thought better of it, and let his arm fall once more.

For what seemed a long time, he sat there naked on the stool, getting colder all the time until he remembered the blanket they had covered him with after the orderlies had removed his tattered filthy uniform for the RAMC doctor. Stiffly, feeling the goo beginning to harden already, he rose and draped the blanket about his shoulders.

Again he sank back into his reverie, his mind blank, hardly aware of his surroundings and the steady pace of the sentry outside.

Gradually his mind began to mull over the events of the past seventy-two hours or so: the slaughter of poor little Jem, the flight from the Kasbah in Teddy's car to Spanish Morocco and the private plane which had flown him to Gibraltar. The authorities had questioned him briefly, the medics had tended to his battered body and then he had been parked down here under guard, with the warning not to speak to anyone before he had been properly debriefed, whatever that meant. Not that he had anyone to talk to – or wanted to do so, if it came to that. It was as if an unseen tap had been opened in his brain and body and every bit of imagination and energy had been drained out of him. He knew he was alive and that things were expected of him sooner or later – why else the intense treatment that he had been given since they had landed in Gib? But, in essence, he wasn't interested in living, or whatever the future brought.

He sat there, slowly feeling the white paste hardening on his skinny, battered, young body. Even his testicles seemed tighter. Outside, the guard paced his beat, a regular stamp back and forth that would, he hoped, soon send him to sleep with its monotony, so that he could escape from his surroundings.

But that wasn't to be. Idly his glance fell on the bottle of beer and the little piles of letters tied up in string at the side of his chair. He was dry; he could have done with a drink of beer. Yet he didn't seem to have the energy to bend down and unscrew the bottle cap. Instead he gazed, as if hypnotized, at the bottle's label. *Spatenbräu, München. Muenchen.* That was German, so much he knew. It meant Munich. He frowned the best he could, with the white paste tugging at his forehead. What was German beer doing here in Gib, he asked himself. It was a puzzle that he couldn't seem to solve, so in the end he gave up on it.

It was then that he saw the address on the first green envelope of the little bundle. Again he couldn't quite take in what it meant. It was in his own writing, still the same sort of schoolboy scrawl he had learned at his prep school, partially obscured by the censor's stamp, with another stamp above in a deep-blue ink.

He stared harder. The envelope was addressed to *Leading Wren Tidmus*, the writing now smeared as if by water, though later he would imagine it was tears instead. But it was the second stamp, in the deep-blue ink, which really caught his attention. By screwing up his eyes he could read it. It stated, *Addressee Deceased – Returned to Sender. APO 345.*

He gasped. Suddenly he felt new energy, a fresh sense of purpose surging through his battered body. It was the letter he had sent to her the day he had arrived in Gib in what now seemed another age. He grabbed for it. Hardly knowing what he was about, he ripped the envelope open and snatched out the cheap bit of wartime paper on which he had written her. *Dear Gloria*, he had begun, and then, forgetting his embarrassment at addressing her so openly, he had gone a stage further. He had scratched out the *Dear Gloria* and replaced it, wondering at his own boldness with *My dearest darling Gloria. I can't tell you where I am, though I think you might guess roughly,* he had continued. *But one thing I can tell you, darling, is that I miss you an awful lot.* Again he had scratched out the words and written over them, *Miss you more than I can really bear* . . .

He stopped short. He could read no more. He guessed that Gloria had been killed in one of those 'tip-and-run' raids, as they were calling them – a couple of German fighter-bombers zooming in under the coastal radar net, dropping their damned bombs and off again before anyone really knew what was going on, leaving behind another handful of shattered bodies. A typical brutish Hun raid, achieving nothing of value, but leaving behind not only the dead but those who would perhaps miss and grieve for the dead for the rest of their lives.

He let his right hand drop, still clutching the letter, which he knew even then signalled the end of another stage of his life. There he sat in the bare room, feeling the white coat of goo hardening and shrinking on his naked body, the silent tears coursing down behind the white mask which now covered his young, sad face.

But even as Smythe grieved and wept, the war machine was beginning to roll again. It took no notice of the sorrows and petty problems of the cannon fodder upon which it fed. What did the planners, those self-important staff officers with their superior airs and smart uniforms, care about humankind? The soldiers were figures they moved about on maps and charts. They would fight and die for 'Point X' and 'Contour 455', giving their precious young lives for a remote place whose very name they didn't know.

Up in that same underground complex, tucked in their office, which measured eight by nine feet, Eisenhower and Clark, both unshaven and baggy-eyed, considered the plan for Operation Torch once again in the light of the new information that Smythe had brought them, and the secret cables flashed to Gibraltar by a worried Murphy in Algiers.

'One thing is clear,' Eisenhower pontificated, Camel clenched between his nicotine-stained fingers as usual, 'and that is that nothing is clear now, dammit!'

Clark nodded. 'From what that young limey has told Intelligence,' he agreed, 'we can't rely on the French under Mast giving us the support they promised me, Ike. Or, to put it another way, these Vichy guys, and seemingly the Krauts,

138

are on to us. They did attempt to seal off the Kasbah after our young Englishman escaped. Why in Sam Hill's name didn't he stop in prison or commit suicide or something?' He pulled a face. 'Anyway, the upshot is we've now to agree on the make-up of the landing force which is to take Algiers, basing our calculations on the premise that Mast might not support us and we face a fight on the shore. Don't you agree, Ike?'

Eisenhower frowned. He had been buddies with Wayne ever since they had been at West Point together. But sometimes Churchill's American Eagle got above himself. After all he, Ike, was Supreme Commander, not Clark. But still the diplomat that he was now becoming in this crazy European world, he kept his tongue curbed and said, 'Yes, I agree, Wayne. And, as we've agreed, General Ryder's Thirty-Fourth Division is unblooded and not really up to an all-out ding-dong fight. We'll have to rely on the limeys. After all –' he gave his fellow general that slow winning ear-to-ear smile of his – 'if there are going to be heavy casualties, they'd better be English rather than American. We don't want the folks back home to learn we're suffering casualties fighting the French, of all people. The President wouldn't like it either. It might affect the election, now that he's going to run for a third term.'

''Kay,' Clark said. 'So Ryder is in charge of the Algiers landings, we've agreed on that with the limeys in London. They've given us two commandos, perhaps twelve hundred men, one trained commando and the other newly formed, but with some battle experience. Then we've got this little limey firebrand Brigadier-General Cass, with his brigade of two regular British Army battalions. And all these leading British troops are going to go in wearing American gear, so that the French think they're Yanks.'

'Hm.' Ike looked thoughtful. Then he made his decision. ''Kay, we'll use this limey Sixth Commando. If there's trouble, it's better we use them.'

'Agreed. And by the way, Ike, we could make use of that kid who escaped from the fort. He might well be able to help the commando if General Mast doesn't come through and we've got to fight for the frigging place. After all, the limeys don't seem to take us Yanks seriously. So if they screw up at this Fort Duperre, it's no skin off'n our nose.'

Ike, a much more sensitive man than his old classmate, told himself that Clark would walk over dead bodies to get his way. Aloud, he said, 'Good idea, Wayne. All right, that's decided. Let's get up top and see if we can talk ourselves into a free stiff drink.' He smiled. 'God, am I dry!'

'Yeah, Ike. I think we deserve it for this night's work.' Clark gave a mock moan. 'Who'd be a general! Christ, what a dog's life it is.' Together they puffed and panted as they jogged up the long underground corridor, as was their wont – it was their only exercise. Everything was solved now. From now onwards, everything else was in the hands of the God of War . . .

Two

'The password of the day,' the metallic voice over the tannoy system announced, 'and you'd better mark it well . . . is going to be *Hi-ho, Silver.* The answer is to be *Away*. Got it?'

Next to Major Ronald of the Sixth Commando, Al, their young American liaison officer, commented, 'It's from a comic book, Smythe. The kind of stuff these drugstore cowboys of ours read.' He sighed. 'After all, we are only a partly organized rabble in new khaki.'

Ronald, the commander of the Sixth Commando, smiled, and Smythe tried to, but failed. He hadn't been in a mood to smile for quite a while now. 'You'll do all right on the day, I think, Al,' he reassured the American, who was his own age, though he did wear a West Point class ring, indicating that he was in the US Army as a regular.

'Now hear this.' The tannoy system crackled into metallic life once more. 'Here is an announcement from the commanding general, General Ryder.' There were moans among the assembled troops, British and their American liaison officers. By now they all knew Ryder, tall and angular and older than any other general who was taking part in the attack. He had last seen action in 1918. But he was still full of 'piss and vinegar', as the Americans said wrily behind his back. Now the man at the tannoy relayed his last message to the troops under his command as they prepared to go into the attack.

'Men, a lot of you are not going to come back from that beach today. But if you don't, remember you have done your duty to God's own country.'

The tannoy went dead again as the general's words sank in, to be greeted by a ribald chorus of wet raspberries and English comments about what the old general could do with 'God's own country'.

Now there was little else for the commandos to do as the landing barges hove into sight ready to convey them to the still silent beach, save to empty their pockets of anything that might identify their unit if they were captured. They were leaving the world of peace, perhaps for good, as they filed forward to drop the sad detritus of their past lives: railway tickets, love letters, tickets for local fêtes, dance halls and the like, which for most of them had made up their previous world.

Dutifully Smythe followed the shuffling line of now subdued commandos. He had nothing to add to the pile, not even a letter from 'Mummy' in Bournemouth. He was going into this new battle with nothing that tied him to a previous existence. All he knew was that he must do his duty and, if he could, pay back his debt of honour to poor old Jem and, in a way, to Gloria too. This last month had brought him a love and a friendship which had endured to death. Now he had nothing save a memory. If he was to die, then it would not matter to anyone really.

He paused as he waited his turn to climb down the swaying nets to the barges below, bobbing up and down on the slight waves. He estimated they had to be some six or seven miles off the coast. To both sides of the capital, which the Americans wanted to be taken by frontal assault, the lights twinkled as if this was a world at peace; no blackout here. He sniffed the already warm air and fancied he could smell the acrid odour of Arab cooking. It seemed, he told himself, that they had achieved complete surprise: the lights were still on and the Arabs were cooking.

Next to him, the big commando major with the ribbon of the Military Cross on the breast of his tunic said, as they waited for the order to clamber over the side, 'Looks as if we've caught the Frenchies with their knickers down.' He added with a mischievous side glance at Al, their American officer, 'I suppose they're waiting for the Yanks to wake them up when they come across with their flags flying and their brass bands belting out Sousa marches.'

Al, who was feeling decidedly queasy at the motion of the ship, now that it had stopped to offload them, could only shake his head and gulp, 'Now, now, Major . . . Remember we're still on the same side.'

The major patted him on his back and said, 'Right you are, Al. Well, here we go.' He swung his leg over the rail and said in the mournful voice of the two characters in ITMA, 'After you, Claude . . . No, after *you*, Cecil.' Then he was climbing down the net expertly, hardly seeming aware of the thirty-odd pounds of equipment he carried on his back together with his tommy gun.

Smythe gave the sick American a hand and then he was clambering down the swaying net too, pausing at the bottom with the water only feet away, calculating when he should launch himself into space and – hopefully – into the crazily swaying boat. Minutes later they were on their way into the silent unknown . . .

Robert Murphy was not a great drinking man – diplomats couldn't afford to be – but this long night he would dearly have loved to have gotten drunk and forgotten the whole bloody business. In his way he had been responsible more than any other civilian save the President for the fact that at this moment some great convoys of 300 ships, carrying 111,000 British and American soldiers, were diverging on scores of landing beaches along a 200-mile stretch of coastline in French North Africa. Now, was this great operation, the US's first real venture into total war since the Japs had attacked Pearl Harbor nearly a year before, going to succeed? If it didn't, America's reputation as a great power would suffer a tremendous blow. would be seen Americans would be seen as full of bluff and bluster but without any real means of striking back effectively at their enemies, though in fact the French weren't their real ones.

Since midnight Murphy had known that the American invaders were in position off Algiers. The consulate's clandestine radio had picked up the BBC's signal in French, '*Allo, Robert . . . Franklin arrive.*' Then 'Robert' himself had alerted his volunteer support groups of loyal French civilians, and they had begun placing discreet little resistance groups around the capital's key points: police posts, power stations, communication centres and the like. Still he didn't know exactly how the French armed forces would react.

143

He had already contacted General Juin, the undersized, one-armed senior officer in Algiers, to whom he had already revealed that there might well be an American attack on North Africa. But after he had calmed the general's rage that the attack was now taking place within hours, he had not got much further with him. 'I have known for a long time that the British are stupid,' Juin had snorted, 'but I have always belived Americans were more intelligent. Apparently you have the same genius as the British for making massive blunders.' And that had been the end of that conversation, which had left Murphy feeling more worried than ever.

Murphy might well have been worried. For at that moment his long-laid plans for capturing Vichy strongpoints at the moment of the great invasion had already begun to go wrong.

Vice-Admiral Mercier had been coming back to his quarters from the Kasbah when his expert eye had spotted that something was wrong. Jo-Jo, the *pied-noir* (though he suspected that the big slimy procuror had more black blood in him than white), had found him a real virgin. She might have been eight or nine, a bit young and totally inexperienced, but that hadn't mattered. What mattered was that she was still a virgin, not one of Jo-Jo's faked virgins, their delightful bald slits doctored with alum powder to make them tight. No, this one was the real thing.

Even as he drove through the capital's dark streets, as tired as he was, he still savoured her cries of pain and moans as he had deflowered her, slowly at first, enjoying every moment of it as her lithe body, devoid of anything to speak of way in the way of breasts, had writhed and slithered under his weight; and then sharp and fast and cruel as his passion had run away with him. It was definitely a night he would long remember. Later, when Jo-Jo brought the pictures of her spreadeagled, bloody, deflowered body, she would join that secret collection he would savour in his old age.

But as he had passed the Villa des Oliviers and had spotted the suspicious group of young men lounging beneath the dim-out street light, he had forgotten the raped Arab girl immediately. He had sensed something was wrong. And he had reacted at once, too. 'Heinz,' he hissed to the driver, another German from the Legion, for these days he trusted the wooden-headed Boches more than he did his fellow countrymen. 'Turn right. Stop and wait for further orders. *Ist das klar?*'

'*Klar, Herr Admiral.*'

The driver swung round the corner, hit the breakes and waited as the admiral pulled the sub-machine gun from beneath the seat. Automatically the German felt for his own pistol. He sensed there was going to be trouble. 'All right, Heinz. Take us back as far as the first light. Then we're going in on foot. Prepared for trouble. *Los!*' Heinz grinned, then took off again.

Softly Mercier opened his door. Crouched low, he moved forward. Like two predatory wolves they advanced on the unsuspecting youths chatting in low voices under the street light and smoking fitfully, still unaware of the other two men.

Now Mercier saw they were armed. One even carried an old World War One rifle over his shoulder, probably a weapon brought back from the trenches by his father. He cursed. There was something seriously wrong here. Had the de Gaullists staged a *coup d'état*? It was always something to reckon with from that fool general in exile in London, being paid his thirty pieces of silver of traitor's money by that fat drunk Churchill.

They came ever closer. Still the men didn't notice them. Mercier stopped. It was time to act; they were close enough. He would catch them off guard, make them think they were dealing with the Boche.

That would make them crap their pants. *Was machen sie hier?*' he demanded in a harsh voice.

They turned round, startled out of their wits.

Mercier raised the sub-machine gun. Naturally he and his driver were hopelessly outnumbered. But that didn't worry the admiral one bit. He was the one who had caught them by surprise; now he wasn't going to allow them to recover. He pressed the trigger. The gun chattered frantically. Glass shattered. A street light went out. Hastily the traitors dropped to the pavement, save the one with the ancient rifle. Heinz didn't give him a chance to use it. He fired from the hip. The slug caught the young man in the stomach. He was propelled violently backwards as if he had been struck in the guts by a

145

gigantic fist. He slammed into the nearest wall, slithering down it, leaving a trail of bright red blood behind him as he slumped to the pavement.

That took the heart out of the would-be rebels. Here and there they started raising their hands above their heads as they squatted there on the pavement, while inside the headquarters lights flicked on everywhere as angry voices cried orders and counter-orders and somewhere sirens began to wail their urgent warning.

While Heinz covered their prisoners, Mercier ran back to the car. He pulled the car phone from its cradle and dialed the emergency code. The duty officer came on at the double as if he had been expecting this urgent call all along. The admiral didn't waste any time. He knew from that terrible dawn at Mers-el-Kebir two years ago that one had to act swiftly and decisively in such situations if one didn't want the rot to spread. 'Call out the Legion. Alert naval command, check with General Juin.' He rapped out his orders in swift, hammer-like staccato phrases. 'This is not a practice drill. Get patrols on the streets immediately.' He gasped for breath and ended with, 'Captain, France and her honour are at stake. We have been attacked. We will defend ourselves!' And even as he spoke the bold, defiant words, he knew he was right. For over at Fort Duperre, the guns manned by the French naval gunners had commenced thundering. The battle for Algiers had begun.

Three

By now half the commandos' assault craft were sinking or were having engine trouble. In the first 'V' of the clumsy barges conveying them to the already smoke-shrouded shore, the commandos' commander was busy with the rest of his men baling out the water with the newfangled American helmets with which they had been issued to fool the French defenders that the attackers were Yanks. 'Only,' he gasped, 'the bloody Frenchies don't care if we're English, Americans or bloody Wailing Dervishes . . . as long as they can ruddy well kill something or other.'

And the '*pompons rouges*' were doing their best to do just that. White tracer zipped lethally across the glowing surface of the sea. Ancient French machine guns, vintage World War One, chattered like irate woodpeckers. As more and more coastal searchlights swept the bay, the gunfire became ever more intense. Cherry-red flame of cannon stabbed the gloom everywhere and the naval gunners were not alone in their attempt to ward off the invasion.

Minesweepers and fast motor launches came zig-zagging out from the harbour at speed to meet the enemy small craft, pumping shells from their quick-firers as they did so. It was, so it seemed to Smythe, as if they were advancing into a solid wall of killing white. Next to him, protected by the steel ram, which was already scarred a shining silver by the hits from the French guns, Al, the American Liaison officer, shouted above the racket, 'Holy mackerel, I never thought it was going to be like this!' The major with the MC gave him a fleeting smile and commented, 'Don't worry, old bean, this is just for openers.' Next moment he ducked, as a glowing white solid-shot shell whizzed over the ramp and took the head off the commando corporal behind him. It rolled, complete with steel helmet, into the scuppers, like a macabre football abandoned by some careless schoolkid. Al's shoulders heaved violently and he started to vomit on the deck. The major with the MC shook his head but made no comment.

But still the barges kept going, braving the shells and small-arms fire, heading straight for the fort, which seemed to be the centre of the French resistance.

Smythe, with his knowledge of navigation and general layout of the Ilot de la Marine, as this stretch of the Algiers' coastline was called, could see they were being carried well off course. The launch which had been supposed to guide them to their objective had been sunk almost as soon as they had left the mother ship. Now, in the general confusion of the assault, with barges sinking everywhere, the three landing craft commanded by the jolly commando major were heading right across the French line of fire. Smythe didn't need to be told how dangerous that was. They were already being bracketed with well-aimed and directed French artillery fire. But at the same time, if they could survive that long, they'd reach the dead ground to the right of Fort Duperre, their objective. Once there, they'd make their attack and, with luck, reach those interior stairs that he and poor Jem had used for their escape. He bit his lip as he thought his new and makeshift plan of attack out.

'Penny for 'em?' the major asked.

Before Smythe could answer, a rocket hit the barge. It rocked violently. They hung on grimly as the barge swayed and, to the rear, commandos went down in a flurry of bloody severed arms and legs, dying before they hit the deck.

'What a mess,' Al managed to gasp. 'What a goddam—' He never finished the sentence. For, once again, hot choking vomit filled his throat at the sight of the grievously wounded commandos trying to walk on bloody, gory stumps of legs severed at the knees.

The major and Smythe ignored the retching man. They had other problems. Besides, Al was young and vital enough to overcome the trauma of this terrible assault. If he didn't, he'd never be of any use to anyone, military or civilian, any more.

Hastily, shouting his makeshift new plan to the commando officer, Smythe finished with, 'A bit of luck, sir, and we might just do it.'

As unflappable as ever, the major said cheerfully, 'Of course we'll do it, Smythe. We're British after all, aren't we? The bash-on spirit and all that, what.'

Despite the danger and instant death all around him, Smythe grinned. The major was a card. Somehow, he thought now, they might well just do it. They sailed on.

Now it was almost light. To the east the sun was a blood-red ball on the horizon. In a few moments, with the suddenness of Africa, the sky would be transformed and it would be full day. Mercier slung his sub-machine gun and nodded his head in approval. Once it was fully light, they'd start mopping up the American invaders and their French running dogs, who, on his orders, were being rounded up by loyal troops all over the city.

Hartmann, laden with grenades and with belts of machine-gun rounds criss-crossed over his broad shoulders, clicked to attention in his usual annoying manner and said, 'Beg to report, sir, Fort Duperre has suffered no casualties. No guns knocked out either. Still possesses fifty shells per gun. More on its way.'

'Excellent, Hartmann. Good news indeed. We'll show these damned arrogant Americans, won't we? They think they can just take us over like that.' He clicked his thumb and fore-finger together loudly.

'Yessir . . . and sir.'

'Yes?'

'The commandant of the fort reports we'll get aerial support from the Maison Blanche Air Base. They're ready to take off now. As soon as it's full daylight, they'll attack.'

Mercier's cruel face lit up. 'Splendid,' he said above the racket. 'It's a pity that the damned English are not among the invaders. This time we could make it Mers-el-Kebir in reverse and sink their fleet. All right, Hartmann, keep close. I'm going to be in need of you. There'll be promotion in this one for you, Hartmann. You deserve it.'

Hartmann beamed. Again the vision of a comfortable sexy

149

retirement, complete with nubile Arabian women and plenty of good Munich 'suds' flashed momentarily before his mind. Then he was hurrying back to the fort to carry out Mercier's instructions. But Sergeant Hartmann, once a member of the communist 'Red Front' organization and now serving his former enemies, the Nazis, was not fated to enjoy that sexy, drunken retirement. He'd be dead before this day was out. Lieutenant Horatio Smythe would see to that . . .

The surviving commandos' luck had changed slightly. Hidden temporarily from the French fire, the battered sinking landing craft were hitting the red sand north of Fort Duperre and discharging their shaken cargoes. But the commandos were recovering rapidly. They knew that the sooner they were off the beach, the longer they would live. They guessed that the French from the fort and elsewhere would probably be looking for survivors of the abortive landing; and from what they had seen of the French defenders already, they thought the French wouldn't be inclined to show much mercy.

With Smythe and the major in the lead, they advanced swiftly up the sloping beach, laden down with weapons and equipment like pack animals, their scouts casting swift glances to left and right for the first glimpse of the enemy. For now all illusions that the French wouldn't fire at them, their 'liberators', had been tossed to one side. The French were as much their enemy as were the Germans.

Now, as they left the beach in little groups of fours and fives, weapons at the ready, prepared to open fire at the first suspicious sign, they began bumping into Arabs, who it was obvious were not one bit inclined to fight. Mostly they wanted to beg, hands outstretched for cigarettes, or squatting – revealing that they were naked under their dirty robes – to pick up the commandos' abandoned cigarette ends. As the major commented, 'Wonder why the Frenchies want to rule a colony made up of this sort? Haven't got a pot to piss in, by the looks of 'em.'

Smythe grunted something, preoccupied as he was with his plan to get into the fort.

They pushed on, to be stopped by a French civilian trying to start a pre-war Panhard, powered by an enormous bag of

150

coal gas, which billowed and quivered like a tethered animal on the roof of the automobile. He looked at the commandos with their blackened faces and said, his English perfect. 'How am I supposed to greet you chaps? Heil Hitler . . . God bless America . . . Or three cheers for the blacks?' Then he saw the English patches on the sleeves of the soldiers and added, 'Or would God save the King be more apt?'

The major frowned. He was in no mood for witty verbal exchanges. He snapped, 'What do you want?'

'I'm stuck, sir. The gas isn't coming through. If I had some help, I think I could get the old thing working again.' He looked at the major and added, 'I was at Oxford, you know.'

Next to Smythe, Al repressed a giggle and said *sotto voce*, 'I say, chaps, anyone for tennis or croquet?'

The major considered for a moment. 'You might be of some use, I suppose.' He raised his voice. 'Sergeant-Major, get a couple of lads and give this old jallopy a push start. We can dump our heavy gear in it.'

A few moments later, the old Panhard was on its way again, puffing and panting laboriously as if it was a live thing. Its rear was packed high with two-inch mortars, bren guns and the rucksacks of those of the commando who had been slightly wounded, while at the front, behind the wheel, the strange Frenchman steered the car at five miles an hour under the suspicious gaze of a troop sergeant-major, possessor of a great bristling dyed-black moustache. Behind came the rest, lightened of their gear, trotting along at the commando's regulation four miles an hour, the men waving happily at the Arabs they passed as if they were on some sort of speed march back home. As Al commented, 'Holy cow, Horatio, what a way to go to war. Are you sure this ain't a Hollywood movie?'

Smythe smiled back, but didn't rise to the bait. This whole business seemed to have been a bloody cock-up ever since that moment the American General Clark had lost his trousers in the surf. Yet somehow, he thought at that moment, with the black dots on the horizon hurrying ever closer, it wasn't going to end in laughter.

Four

The commandos were taking the speed march in their stride; they had done them often enough. But Al, and to a certain extent Smythe, weakened by his recent prison experience, were flagging. They were dropping further and further behind the commandos, who seemingly were only too eager to get into action.

Al gasped, 'I think we're doing right being here. But look at that Frog in the car.' He indicated the Oxford-educated Frenchman. 'Does he seem to care what we're doing for his country? I mean, does he look as if he regards us as liberators?'

Smythe swallowed hard and fought for breath. He looked at the American, his handsome, clean-cut face lathered in sweat, and told himself that he supposed he had been the same sort of innocent, sent out into the real world for the first time, the day he had passed out from Dartmouth. The 'King-Emperor', the 'hearts of oak, jolly tars' sort of patriotism, 'all that red on the map,' of the British Empire 'on which the sun never sets', and so on. The recent months of hard action and suffering had taught him things weren't that way at all.

Al, however, still retained his innocence, a different kind, of course, a sort of peculiar American innocence, believing his country was the best in the world; that 'Yankee get up and go' was the ideal that would save the rest of the non-American world. Al wouldn't – couldn't – realize that much of the world didn't believe in American values, that is, if the rest of the world really knew what those values were, apart from making a lot of money.

'Perhaps he's right, Al,' Smythe gasped. 'About not regarding us as liberators.'

Al laughed shortly. 'You might be right. But you think they'd want to be free of the Krauts – and those Arabs, I bet they wouldn't mind a deal with us. We could give them a better kind of life than the piss-poor one they lead now.'

Smythe shrugged again. 'We'll see, Al. Main thing is that we get this job done and come out of it in one piece, eh?'

'Guess you're right, Horatio. But I promised my mom before I shipped overseas that I—' His words were drowned by the snarl of a plane coming in fast behind them. They swung round as one. A fighter was roaring in at tree-top height, its prop wash thrashing the cropped, burnt grass back and forth. Purple lights crackled the length of its wing. Smythe gave the startled American a push. He toppled over, crying, 'What the shit is going on, Horatio?' as a line of bullets erupted the length of the road, digging up the hard clay, hurrying furiously towards the car with its billowing bag of gas on its roof.

'Watch your ears!' Horatio cried, clapping his hands to his own ears, as the French fighter flashed over them, dragging its evil black shadow behind them.

The plane's last burst slammed into the gas bag. Desperately the French driver twisted the wheel. Too late! The gas bag punctured. Next moment it exploded with a roar and flash of bright red flame, and the sergeant-major and the Frenchman were falling into the drainage ditch, a mass of flames.

The fighter soared into the morning sky, dragging a white tail behind it as it gave the victory roll and then, levelling out, came in again at tree-top height. This time, however, the French pilot wasn't going to have it all his own way. 'Fire at the bugger!' the enfuriated major yelled above the ear-splitting racket of the plane and burning car. To emphasize his order, he whipped out his revolver and started blazing away at the approaching plane. His two leading bren gunners needed no urging, as they saw the sergeant-major stagger out of the ditch, one blackened claw groping in front of him like that of a blind man, his face looking as if someone had just thrown a handful of black jam at it. The number two bent hastily. The gunner slapped his light machine gun across the other's back and opened fire at once. Tracer zipped upwards in a lethal morse. At that range, the commando gunner couldn't miss. The perspex cockpit splintered into a glittering spider's web. Blinded, the pilot tried frantically to keep control. Smythe could see his fear-crazed, contorted face. He threw up his hands as if in despair as the plane slammed into the ground fifty yards away and shuddered like a live thing, giving up the ghost.

Minutes later, when they were satisfied that the Morane fighter was not going to burst into flames, they approached the plane, its prop smashed backwards like a peeled banana skin, the pilot dead, skewered neatly through the stomach by his own joystick, the only sound the dripping of leaking hot oil. The commandos stared at the wrecked plane as if bewildered, until the man who had shot it down said, 'The sod deserves what he got. Look at the fuselage just under the cockpit, mates.'

Smythe peered over the head of the soldier in front of him as the men crowded around the plane and gasped. Three red-white-and-blue roundels were painted there: the roundels of the Royal Air Force.

'Cor, ferk a duck!' a commando exclaimed. 'The Frog sod has gone and shot some of our own blokes down. Them's his victories. Would yer bloody believe it! Frogs killing our own brylcreem boys!'

Smythe remembered now the stories of the French Air Force fighting against British troops in Syria and bombing Gibraltar after they had surrendered to the Germans . . . and the British bombardment of the French Navy at Mers-el-Kebir, just down the road from where they were at this very moment.

The major with the MC said softly, almost thoughtfully, 'Don't think about it, chaps. At least we know now where we stand with our former allies. They're going to put up a fight for it after all. It's not going to be a walkover. Come on, let's get the digit out of the orifice.' Minutes later, they were on the move again, marching this time in battle formation, with every man holding his trigger finger poised, waiting for the inevitable, and the French . . .

The commando major was right. The French were fighting back, and this was not a token resistance. This was a bitter struggle, where no quarter would be given to the men who were landing, believing the French owed them a favour, a debt to be paid back for what the US Army had done for France in 1918. French aircraft from Maison Blanche were here, there and everywhere, bombing and strafing the invasion's fleet and the few barges which had managed to reach the beach intact. But it was not only the American and pseudo-American infantry who were being attacked by the French, the ships of the Royal Navy which had brought them there were under attack from air and land by their one-time ally.

The Royal Navy skippers had refused to fly the Stars and Stripes. More than one of them had declared, against orders, 'If we fight, we do so under the White Ensign.' Now they suffered for their patriotism and loyalty to their service.

Already two British small craft were blazing from end to end, riddled by French shore batteries, their decks littered with dead and dying sailors. Another, commanded by a young destroyer captain, had berthed to land infantry of the US Army's premier infantry division, 'the Big Red One', the First Division. He had not stayed at the first berth long. The French had moved up light artillery pieces along the quay and had proceeded to fire at the destroyer over open sights. Hastily he shifted his berth again – and yet again. But both times the French field artillery and coastal batteries were after him at once, slamming shell after shell into the destroyer's thin steel sides till they gleamed silver with the shells' impact, and the destroyer's superstructure was a chaotic mess of jumbled gantries and fallen masts. In the end he gave the order to withdraw. It was either that or lose his ship and all aboard her.

Behind he left 250 bewildered infantrymen of the 'Big Red One', which boasted 'there's the Big Red One and then the rest of the US Army'. For a while they tried to form a defensive position. But it didn't work.

While the destroyer sank as it was being towed away from the scene by another British ship, and the bells from Algiers' Catholic cathedral started to peal, summoning the faithful to Sunday Mass, the 250 infantry of the First Division gave up. They had trained long for this invasion: the liberation of the French 'from the crushing Nazi yoke', as their President had just declared over national radio back home. Now they raised their hands in surrender – *to the French*!

Murphy despaired. His whole carefully prepared plan had collapsed. Mast had disappeared. The promises he had made at the Teissier house had failed to materialize. His own measures to contain the French hardliners had come to naught as well. Admiral Mercier, that cunning dog who controlled French Intelligence in Algiers had seen to that. With his usual efficiency and speed, he had rounded up virtually every anti-Vichy, pro-American French group in the capital and put them behind bars. Now it was clear that not only was Darlan's French Navy resisting the invasion, but also the Army and Air Force, some of the latter's pilots taking off without orders to attack the Allied fleet which lay offshore at anchor, ready for the taking.

Murphy sucked his teeth and for the second time this fateful Sunday morning, he wished he could swallow a couple of stiff drinks. They might well tip him into that oblivion that he sought. But that wasn't to be, he knew. He had been party to creating this mess, though he had warned FDR that it might happen like this. But he knew the President. He never admitted to a mistake. If things went really bad, he, Murphy, would be the guy left holding the crock of shit.

He sat there, thinking what he might do to save the situation, and naturally his own neck too, while, outside, the guns thundered and the French fighters dived and swooped down to rooftop height, looking for further prey. He told himself he could not trust any of the French officers, such as Mast and Juin. They wouldn't make a move in the right direction until they knew that their own position was secure. He pulled a bitter face at the thought. Their pensions were more important to them than the honour of France. What he needed now was someone who could sway the French Navy in the right direction: someone cynical and ambitious, who would be prepared to carry out any kind of 'piggery', as the Frogs called it, as long as he could feather his own nest.

Again Mercier's cunning, cynical face flashed before his mind's eye. He knew that although the head of French Naval Intelligence was a rabid supporter of Admiral Darlan, and through him the Vichy government that had made the little admiral a senior member of the cabinet, like all of them, Mercier was on the make. But what would bring him over to the Allied side? It had to be something very important and lucrative. But what?

Even as Murphy puzzled out that overwhelming problem, and bad news about the invasion came flooding into the consulate, things were changing. At eight o'clock, with the Anglo-Americans being repulsed by stiff French resistance virtually everywhere in the capital, the most alarming news yet was brought in to Murphy by a flustered signals clerk. 'Sir,' he quavered. 'I thought you'd better see this immediately.' Even before Murphy could snap that he had better things to do than read State Department routine signals, the clerk thrust it into his hands and stepped back hastily, as if he half-expected his boss to hit him once he had read the message.

Indeed, Murphy's normally ruddy complexion turned an ugly white as his eyes flicked along the lines of the signal, which read: *Radio Vichy has just announced that Admiral Darlan is now in Algiers. His son has apparently been stricken with polio. No way to confirm this. Petain has given Darlan permission to visit his son, Alain. In the light of the current situation in French North Africa, Darlan has taken over the defence.*

Murphy groaned out loud and the clerk fled. Admiral Darlan, the fervent anglophobe and enemy of all who associated with the English, was now in charge here in Algiers. The news couldn't be worse. Murphy buried his head in his hands and felt he might burst into tears at any moment now.

Five

'All right, Corporal,' the major commanded. 'See what you can do to the buggers with the Piat.'

'Sir,' the big burly corporal responded immediately. He started crawling forward to the fort, lugging the strange anti-tank weapon, which looked like a sawn-off leg and foot, behind him.

Above them the French garrison were still firing odd shots in the hope of hitting one of the attackers, as they had been doing since they had first spotted the advance guard of the commando. But now the British were in the dead ground, the French riflemen on the roof had little hope of hitting their attackers.

Next to Smythe, crouching in the cropped grass, an excited Al, .45 pistol at the ready, asked over the angry snap-and-crack of small-arms fire, 'What's he going to do with that ugly-looking thing, Horatio?'

Smythe answered, 'I don't know much about infantry weapons, Al. It's an anti-tank weapon to be used by infantry against armour really. I've seen a practice drill with it once. Has a kick like a mule. But whether the missile will penetrate stone and concrete is anybody's guess.'

'And if it does?'

The major answered Al's question for him, as the corporal fixed the pear-shaped bomb into the muzzle of the ugly-looking weapon. 'We call it mouse-holing. If we can blast a hole in the outer wall, then we'll move on to the next wall and hope-fully capture the garrison on the hop. That's where you come in, Lieutenant Smythe. You can guide us to the heart of the fort.' He looked grim as the corporal tucked the padded base of the Piat securely into his right shoulder and squinted down

158

the sight. 'The sooner we capture this fort, the better it will be for our poor chaps out there in the bay. They seem to be taking one hell of a beating.'

The two younger officers looked solemn too, but they said nothing as they watched the big corporal prepare to fire. Next instant he did so. There was a hellish boom. For a moment they could see the missile flying from the Piat's muzzle, the next the corporal was sprawled on his back, thrown there by the shock of that powerful discharge.

They waited. Not for long. The anti-tank missile slammed against the fort's wall. Concrete cracked, splinters flying from the point of impact, fissures running in every direction in a crazy spider's web. Anxiously they waited for the smoke to clear.

When it did, the major swore angrily, 'Christ Almighty, we've hardly dented the bloody wall! Can you see?'

The other two could. There was a hole in the fort's wall, but it hadn't penetrated right through, and the major said, 'I can't risk my men working on that hole to break through. As soon as they hear them working with their bayonets and entrenching tools, the Frenchies on the roof will be on to them. And it won't be raining pennies from heaven, I can tell you, gentlemen.'

Neither Al nor Smythe laughed at the major's attempt at humour. The situation was too serious for that. Out in the bay, yet another British destroyer had been hit by the French coastal batteries and was limping away, making smoke to cover its withdrawal.

It was then that Smythe made his suggestion. Eagerly the major listened to his bold plan, constantly throwing glances at the waterfront beyond the fort, as if trying to assess whether they should go ahead with the younger officer's suggestion or retreat while there were still time and ships to take them off the beach . . .

Pulling himself together, Murphy finally made *his* decision. He knew that when it came out what he was about to do, there'd be a hell of an outcry in the States, and more so in Britain, especially among de Gaulle's Free French based there.

If it went badly wrong, naturally President Roosevelt would ask for his resignation. But he knew FDR. People said that he played his cards so close to his chest that the ink rubbed off them on to his shirt. As long as such things didn't affect his chances of being re-elected, he'd go along with Murphy's decision. After all, he was the man who had decided to invade French North Africa. It was his baby. He would want the invasion to succeed, even if it meant dealing with pro-German French fascists.

As soon as he had recovered from the shock of finding that Darlan was in Algiers and had taken over command in North Africa, Murphy had phoned one-armed General Juin to sound him out on the drastic new situation. Juin had expressed sympathy with the Allied cause. But now he was resolutely sitting on the fence. As he said to Murphy, 'He can immediately countermand any orders I give, Mr Murphy. If Darlan does that, the lower echelons will obey his orders and not mine.' And that was that. He'd get no more out of General Juin, that hero of World War One.

For a long while he considered why Darlan had turned up in North Africa at this juncture. Was it just on account of his son's illness? Or was there something else behind it? Had he noted the way the wind was blowing now that the Americans had entered the war and Germany had been defeated in Libya by the British, and in Russia, too? This November of 1942, there were a lot of leading Frenchmen – politicians and soldiers – who were secretly changing sides in order to save their own necks just in case the Anglo-Americans might win the war. Was Admiral Darlan one of them?

Now Murphy had made up his mind. As he left the Consulate in his big US Buick to go to the police post of the Villa des Oliviers, where he guessed Darlan would be, together with General Juin, he had thought the unthinkable. In the name of the United States, he would try to make a deal with Darlan which would save the invasion.

Even as he rode there, he remembered all the charges that would be levelled against him if he pulled it off and the deal became public. Darlan had used Vichy airports in Syria to supply Rommel, and had done the same for the Iraqi rebels

160

fighting the British in that area. He'd ordered Gibraltar bombed and would have done the same to London, if Mussolini's air force hadn't beaten Darlan to it – and suffered a very bloody nose in the process. Worse still, as far as the US Jewish media were concerned, Darlan had introduced the Nazi anti-semitic laws into French North Africa, which had resulted in French citizens of Jewish blood being arrested and imprisoned. As the Buick began to approach the mustard-coloured Villa des Oliviers, guarded by gigantic Senegalese sentries with their tarbushes and ritually scarred faces, he stopped himself thinking about what might happen if he came to some agreement with the French admiral. First do the deal and if it resulted in victory for the Americans in their first major venture overseas, then he might just get away with it. As he stepped out of the car and showed his ID to the giant sentry, he crossed his fingers behind his back. Then he entered what he now considered was the lion's den . . .

Cautiously Smythe approached the hidden door in the wall, followed by Al and two commandos, their tommy guns at the ready. Behind them a bren gunner was firing repeated short bursts at the roof to stop any French rifleman venturing to the parapet to see what was going on below.

Smythe paused. With the borrowed bayonet he tested the mortar to find out where the door was. The last time he had done this, it had been at night and in darkness. But in broad daylight it was still a difficult task, for the door was completely flush with the wall. Angrily, trying to avoid any noise, he tested and tested for the catch that would open the wall door. But the opening stubbornly refused to reveal itself. It was just when he was about to give up that the tip of the bayonet's blade caught and the door opened slightly to emit that odour of stale air and animal droppings that he remembered from the night when Jem had been killed so cruelly. He signalled to the others to move forward and stepped in, blinded after the sunshine outside. There was that clawed scuttle of fleeing rats that had happened before, and then he was ascending the dusty steps, hand holding his revolver, suddenly wet with a tense sweat. Behind him the other three did the same.

When he came level with the cell-block floor, he paused and listened. Behind him the others tensed on the stairs, holding their breath. They knew if they were discovered on the steps, they were dead. The French would fire first and ask questions later. But Smythe could hear nothing. He nodded and they started crawling higher.

As Smythe had planned it, they would climb to the roof, deal with the handful of French up there, hoping that they would surrender and not put up a fight. Once that was done, and perhaps using whatever captives they had as a human shield, they would work their way through the interior, from floor to floor, taking prisoners as they went, till they reached the main door. Once there, they'd form a small defensive perimeter till the rest of the commandos had entered to do their job.

'Well, it's not a plan that would earn you a commendation at staff college,' the major had commented when Smythe had explained it to him. 'But it does have the element of surprise. The best o' luck,' he added with the kind of irony that Al said he could never understand. 'And if it doesn't work out, Smythe, do try and make a handsome corpse. We do want a tidy show, don't we, old chap, eh?'

Now they were closer to the centre of the fort, and the intruders could hear the rumble of guns firing out across the bay at the invading fleet, and the whine and rattle of the trolleys bringing up more shells from the arsenal below. It was noise for which they were grateful. It covered any that they might make.

Now Smythe judged, as the firing of the guns became more subdued, that they were approaching the roof and the exit he and Jem had used that night. He turned and whispered to the others. 'We'll be going out in half a mo. Once we're out on the roof, no messing. If anyone makes a wrong move, don't bugger about – *shoot him!*'

Behind him, Al, looking very worried now, nodded.

Smythe gave him a quick smile of encouragement. After all, this was the young American's first taste of action. Naturally he was apprehensive about what was to come. Behind him the two burly commandos showed no emotion whatsoever, save that of determination, their hard faces keen and determined. Smythe knew he could rely upon them.

He took a deep breath and counted to three, as the others watched him, waiting for the signal. '*Three!*' He pushed the door. It opened easily — and noiselessly. Spread along the roof, lying on their stomachs, there were some six or seven sailors, their flat caps adorned with the red *pompons* thrust to the backs of their heads, as they snapped off shots to left and right, though at whom they were firing, Smythe hadn't the faintest idea. But he was glad they were. Thus they were too preoccupied to notice the four men emerging from the staircase between the inner and outer wall.

Smythe didn't hesitate. In his beat prep-school French, he yelled, '*Assez . . . Ça suffit . . .*' The words died on his lips as a burly, well-remembered figure emerged from behind the concrete ventilation shaft in the middle of the roof, machine gun tucked under his brawny arm as if it were a kid's toy.

He grinned, in no way shocked by the sight of the intruders in their foreign uniform. Then he saw Smythe. He recognized him immediately. 'Ach, the little Englishman,' he sneered in German. 'Come for another visit to Sergeant-Major Hartmann, eh?' He raised the machine gun, while Symthe stared back at him as if mesmerized, unable to move.

Behind him, the two commandos crouched. They were still jammed in the narrow door, unable to fire. 'Move it, sir,' the bigger of the two cried. 'Ferk a duck, sir, *move!*'

Still Smythe couldn't. But Al, his face pale and glazed with sweat, could. As a smirking Hartmann curled his finger round the trigger of the machine gun, the knuckles whitening as he prepared to fire, the young American stepped into the open, ignoring the danger, and raised his Colt, crouching a little, like a western gunslinger in a Hollywood movie, teeth bared.

Six

Admiral Darlan was a small man. Now stumpy and pigeon-breasted, he strode back and forth as if he were half a metre taller, never taking his shifty eyes off Murphy. No wonder, the latter told himself, that his staff called the Frenchman 'Popeye', after the comic-book character. Murphy shortened his stride to keep pace with the little admiral, insisting time and time again, 'The moment has now arrived, Admiral, to come over to us. *Please.*'

Darlan took his pipe out of his weak, slack lips, the blood-red lips of a sensualist. 'I cannot break my word to Marshal Petain now,' he said. 'I have given him my oath. But I will radio Vichy for guidance, Mr Murphy.'

Murphy gave a little sigh of relief. He was getting somewhere at last.

'Let us go outside now, Mr Murphy, and get a breath of fresh air while the message to Vichy is prepared.'

The message was ready before they could do so, and Murphy told one of his 'apostles' to take it downtown and have it radioed to France immediately. But the 'apostle' was made of sterner stuff than his boss. Outside, he opened Darlan's message and found it not to his liking. With a grunt, he tore it up and threw the pieces away and called out his own men. Thus it was that when Murphy, accompanied by Juin and Darlan, finally came outside, they found the giant Senegalese guards had been replaced. Instead of the black soldiers, they were confronted by some fifty civilians, armed and wearing the armband of the Free French Forces, de Gaulle's own organization.

Murphy now changed his tack. 'Admiral,' he announced. 'In an hour's time, General Clark, America's most senior

164

officer in this area, will be landing at Maison Blanche airfield. He will come with orders from General Eisenhower, the allies' Supreme Commander. Those orders are to achieve a general armistice in French North Africa, come what may.' He looked pointedly at the little admiral.

Darlan's face paled. He blustered, 'But this is an outrage! I shall order this General Clark of yours arrested immediately, if he sets one foot on French soil.' But Darlan's words were without conviction and Murphy felt a renewed sense of hope. Darlan was weakening. Perhaps he, Murphy, could save the invasion yet. Now he snapped, not knowing whether he had the authority to do so or not, or even whether he might be imprisoned in a Vichy jail before the day was out, 'Admiral, it may be *you* who will land in jail if you don't agree to what we intend.' Not wanting to push his luck any further, he continued with, 'Now I suggest we drive out to Maison Blanche airfield to meet General Clark.'

Surprisingly enough, Darlan and then Juin agreed.

With the firing still going on in the distance and Spitfires ferried from a British aircraft carrier offshore overhead, Clark's massive B-17 began to roll down the Maison Blanche runway to come to a stop opposite the colonel of the Signal Corps whose job it was to photograph the arrival of the conquering hero.

The colonel, Darryl F. Zanuck, who had once written the scripts for the dog movie series *Rin Tin Tin*, and who had left his job as a senior executive of Twentieth Century Fox, knew exactly what was expected of him. Indeed, he had already roughly scripted the arrival with Clark before his four-engined bomber had left Gibraltar. Although Clark had carefully worn his helmet throughout the flight from Gibraltar, just in case the B-17 was attacked, he wanted to be shown leaving the plane in his garrison cap. That would demonstrate to the folks back home just how little he cared for his own safety. Thereafter he must be shown before the Stars and Stripes flag, emphasizing his patriotism, before he gave a short speech to the press, if the Signal Corps could find any pressmen who spoke English in time. If not, it had to be GIs, preferably dusty and battle-worn, but visibly happy at their victory.

Now, as Murphy and the French waited and a few reluctant GIs who had deserted their outfit to loot the Maison Blanche's wine and beer store were being forced towards the runway by MPs, the broken bottles behind them marking their progress, the plane came to a stop. Colonel Zanuck, dressed in breeches and riding boots and wearing dark glasses beneath a tropical helmet, so that he looked more like a 20s old-time movie director than an officer in the US Army, yelled, 'Roll 'em,' and Clark came through the door. He paused at the top of the gangway, looking every inch the bold conqueror. Slowly, for the benefit of the whirring cameras, he turned to left and right, as if surveying some battlefield. Then he focused first on the half-drunk GIs, who were trying to look like victorious combat troops, and then on the French delegation. Carefully Zanuck directed the cameras to take a close-up of the undersized Darlan, who looked ridiculous in his overlarge white cap, heavy with gold braid, and the pipe sticking out of the side of his slack mouth, staring up at the noble craggy warrior features of Churchill's 'American Eagle'.

After what seemed an age, Clark moved. He waved the English officer's swagger-stick which he now affected, signalling Murphy and his group to approach closer. Murphy did so quickly. He was glad someone else was taking over this intolerable situation. The French followed more reluctantly, till Clark waved his stick to urge them to greater speed.

Then, once he had them grouped neatly for Zanuck and his cameramen at the bottom of the ladder, he addressed them loftily in the manner of the great conqueror. 'What you are doing now involves the killing not only of Americans, but also Frenchmen. It is time that this bloody business was stopped.'

Darlan knew he had met his match, but still he tried to retain his independence of action. 'I have sent a telegram to Vichy—'

'Stop!' Clark snapped. He waved his stick at Darlan as if shooing away an irritating insect. 'We haven't time for that. I'm going to stand firm on this matter. I know, Admiral, that deep down in your heart you want an end to the fighting.'

Darlan looked as if he really preferred to keep on killing Americans, especially the one towering above him, lecturing

166

him as if he were a damned midshipman and not a five-star Admiral of the Fleet, but he didn't attempt to interrupt. Clark was looking straight into the camera now, following Zanuck's every instruction. The damned American appeared to be more concerned with his image being recorded for posterity than the situation in hand.

Finally, however, Clark forgot the cameras and turned to Darlan once more. This time he displayed that arrogance which would become ever more evident as US military power grew in strength in Europe as the war proceeded, with American generals giving the orders and Europeans snapping to and doing what was expected of them – or else. 'I can't put up with any more delay. This cannot go on. Admiral Darlan, I will have to take you into protective custody without communication if you don't order a ceasefire.'

Darlan's mouth dropped open. He nearly lost his pipe. 'But ...' he commenced, as Murphy started to translate for him. Clark was not prepared to listen. With the new-found arrogance of these US generals, who only months before had been lowly majors and colonels whose future would be a slippered retirement in some cheap and warm part of the United States, he snapped, 'Well, what is it going to be? Co-operation or imprisonment?'

Darlan's fat shoulders slumped. 'But Marshal Petain—'

Again Clark shut him up. 'Petain is a mouthpiece of Hitler. Your answer!'

Darlan gave in. 'Co-operation,' he mumbled.

Clark smiled in triumph. 'Good. Let's get on the stick and stop this damned fighting.' He turned to Murphy. 'Mr Murphy,' he said more politely. 'If you can arrange it, we want a flag-bearing party, a band – *American*, of course – and a few GIs for the armistice ceremony.'

'Better have a few Frogs, too, General,' Zanuck called. 'Looks good for the movie audiences back in the States if we have happy Frogs cheering our boys.'

'Got you, Colonel.' He turned to a somewhat bewildered Murphy, who had never arranged anything like this before, though he'd do it often enough in the years to come. 'Mr Murphy, guess we'd better get on the stick. We don't want too many more of our boys getting killed. Won't look good back home.' With that he went inside the plane and returned wearing a steel helmet for his journey into the city. He was not going to take any risks.

Darlan went back to Algiers with Murphy, who had just been handed a brief message for transmission to the Supreme Commander by Clark. It read, in the private code used by the two former West Point classmates, 'THE YBSOB'S* AGREED'. Now, as they moved off, a shaken Darlan said, 'Mr Murphy, could I ask a favour?'

'Certainly.'

'It's this. Would you mind suggesting to Major-General Clark that I am a five-star admiral. He should stop talking to me like a simple lieutenant.'

At any other time, Murphy might have smiled or even chuckled at such a request, coming from such an important figure as Darlan. But not now. Darlan was finished. It didn't seem fair to rub his nose in the dirt now. 'Of course I will, Admiral.'

'Thank you, Mr Murphy,' Darlan said with what little dignity he had left. '*Vous êtes tres gentil.*'

They parted. For a moment or two Murphy watched the admiral go. He didn't feel sorry of the pudgy little man. He had played a double game for far too long, and he had lost. He was already yesterday's man, passing into history, and Murphy was always interested in how such people, victims of their own hubris, ended up. Then Darlan disappeared from sight. Within the month, he would be dead, the victim of an assassin, whether French, British or American, no one would ever find out . . .

Now, all over Algiers, Vichy officers who had abruptly become 'Americans', as they called those who supported the American invasion, were turning against their former chief, Marshal Petain. They drove at breakneck speed, sirens wailing, to and fro all over the capital, eager to display their new loyalty by ordering their men to cease firing, lay down their arms and welcome their enemies of a couple of hours before as their

*The yellow-bellied son-of-a-bitch.

168

liberators, even allies. For already the Germans were pouring troops from Tunis into Algeria, and the first opposition they would meet were the Vichy French on the border between the two territories. It seemed that the French were now prepared to fight their 'friends' of the last two years, since their defeat at the hands of those self-same Boche in 1940.

But behind these new friendships between Americans and Frenchmen, with generals on both sides exchanging medals, kissing one another, having oriental-style banquets, complete with cous-cous and sheep's eyes, parades, joint flag ceremonies and all the colourful trappings of regular military life, there was a hard truth that was never to be revealed to 'the folks back home'.

Behind the gallant trappings of this new Franco-American military friendship there lay the very unpicturesque dead. About one thousand of them, five hundred British and five hundred American. They had come to liberate the French from the yoke of Nazi tyranny. Or so they had been told. But the Hollywood type of propaganda* they had been fed before the invasion had been all wrong. The French liked the lives they had led in North Africa, whether it had been occupied by the Boche or not. Now, for a goodly while at least, they could continue to enjoy those same pleasures, courtesy of the US Army.

But the infantrymen who had done the fighting – and the dying – to 'liberate' French North Africa would leave behind a memorial that was different. It was exactly six feet of hard, sun-baked African earth. Once planted there, far from their homelands, these 'liberators' were speedily forgotten. Naturally, in the interests of Franco-American solidarity.

*The day before Eisenhower had set sail for North Africa, he had enjoyed, so it was said, a film show. It was Bogart and Bergman's *Casablanca*: that saccharine homage to a doomed Franco-American love affair in Nazi-occupied North Africa.

169

Seven

'**A**l, *stop*!' Smythe cried urgently to the young American, stood out there on the roof, seemingly completely unaware of how close he was to death, with Hartmann preparing to pull the trigger.

Al didn't seem to hear. He remained at the half crouch, legs spread, Colt in hand, as if this really was some sort of movie shoot-out, daring the 'bad guy' in the black stetson to go for his pistol first.

Hartmann might have been bad, but he was no Hollywood gunslinger, adhering to some sort of crazy western code of conduct. The Hartmanns of this hard world had no such beliefs. All they believed in was their own survival.

The big German sergeant-major laughed, as if he had just seen something very funny. Next instant he gave a grunt and took final pressure. Al still did not move. He was too young and inexperienced to recognize the final danger signals which indicated sudden violent death. When he did and cocked his own pistol, it was too late.

Hartmann fired. The sudden chatter of the machine gun shook Smythe. He sprang to his feet and aimed. Al started to crumple, not a sound escaping his abruptly gaping mouth. It was as if he had been trained not to admit pain. Not Hartmann. He was laughing uproariously. It was as if he thought it the greatest joke on earth to see the young American dying on his feet as he slid slowly to the ground. Not for long. Smythe's slug caught him squarely in his fat gut. He screamed. The machine pistol tumbled from his big paws. He grabbed for his shattered stomach, trying to keep his guts from flowing out. Dark red blood welled between his clasped fingers. '*Bitte*,' he choked, as Smythe pointed his pistol again and, on

170

the ground, Al began to die. *'Nicht schiessen . . . ne tirez pas
. . . bitte—'*

The plea died on his lips, as Smythe fired. The bullet
smashed into his chest. He was thrown backwards, as if he
had just been punched by a gigantic fist. Smythe sprang over
a dying Al, carried away by an atavistic bloodlust, a frenzied
madness, an overwhelming desire to slaughter.

Hartmann looked up at him pleadingly, unable to talk now.
Smythe towered over his former torturer, cold, yet wild with
rage. He stared down at the German. 'Die, you swine,' he
heard himself say, his voice seeming to come from far away.
Hartmann tried to raise himself. Smythe didn't give him a
chance to do so. He fired again. Hartmann's spine arched like
a taut bow. Next moment he fell back again, dead.

Now the commandos flooded on to the roof, as the awed
French sailors and handful of soldiers up there raised their
hands and stared at the black-faced British, flicking glances
every now and again at the two dead men sprawled out in
circles of their own blood, with the flies already buzzing
around their faces, seeking nourishment.

Numbly Smythe walked back to the dead American. He
waved away the buzzing flies and stared down at him. The
American's face was relaxed. Whatever grimace had been on
his young clean-cut features at the moment of death had
vanished now, and for a fleeting moment Smythe wondered
at how innocent the dead Al looked. It was as if he had gone
through life protected by the American way of life, without
any of the cares and doubts that afflicted the natives of other
less fortunate cultures. Then he heard the commando major
shout something. He awoke from his momentary reverie.
Hastily he closed Al's eyes and hurried forward to the exit
from the roof, away from the glare of the African sun into the
gloom below. He expected trouble, as did the two commandos
behind him, feeling their way down the stone stairs cautiously,
weapons at the ready. But they encountered none. They
approached the top floor, nostrils assailed by the odour of the
coarse rough *pinot* which was part of the French soldiers' and
sailors' daily ration. Now they could hear the subdued sound
of many voices. Smythe nodded to the two commandos. They

nodded back, raising their weapons, fingers white on their triggers as they took first pressure. They were battle-experienced troopers. They knew what to do.

Smythe paused at the side of the door, revolver raised, hammer cocked. The smell of cheap wine had grown ever stronger. Something strange was going on, but he couldn't guess what. After all, this was a garrison under siege. Why would they be drinking wine at this stage of the game? 'Well, get in there, man,' a little voice at the back of his mind rasped, 'and bloody well find out.'

He hesitated no longer. He sprang forward and went through the open door – and stopped dead. There were sailors and soldiers everywhere, drinking out of their metal canteens and, in some cases, straight from the bottle. They lounged against the walls. Others actually lay on the stone floor. And all were without their weapons, which were stacked against the wall or thrown carelessly to one side. He gasped. Only minutes ago they had been fighting all out, firing at the Allied invaders. Now it seemed they had forgotten the war, despite the fact that they must have known that the enemy was at the gate.

For a moment he was at a loss for words, as he stared dumbfounded at them. It seemed to take an age for someone to break that heavy silence. Finally a bearded sergeant of infantry, drinking *rouge* straight from his steel helmet, chuckled drunkenly, and exclaimed quite happily, or so it seemed to a perplexed Smythe, '*Bienvenu, Monsieur le Rosbif.*'

The remark appeared to be very amusing to the rest. They broke out into loud laughter, repeating the sergeant's welcome cry as if it was the greatest of jokes.

Just as the major with the MC pushed himself into the room, the bigger of the two commandos exclaimed, 'Well, I'll go to your house. They're all bloody barmy.'

'I hope they are, Jenkins,' the major agreed. 'Make our job easier. We don't want any more of the men buying it like that poor young Yank up there. Smythe?'

'Sir?'

'Do you think you can carry on a bit while I deal with this little lot in here. You do know your way about, after all.' He looked pointedly at Smythe. He knew what the younger officer had suffered in this place, and in this indirect manner was giving him a chance to take his revenge.

'Gladly, sir, if I can take your two chaps with me.' Abruptly Smythe remembered Jem and now poor old Al, the American. Their deaths had to be avenged and he knew exactly who should pay the price for their deaths and even that of Gloria Tidmus.

'Of course, off you go – and watch your back. There's something mighty strange going on here. Have you noticed that our own guns out to sea have stopped firing?'

Smythe hadn't. Not that he was interested at the moment. Now his mind was full, even crazy, with the desire for revenge. Before his mind's eye, the cruel face of Vice-Admiral Mercier loomed ever larger.

He gripped his pistol tighter and started for the door, followed by the commandos. Behind him the major shouted a warning. 'Watch your step, Smythe. You never know with the Frogs. Funny lot. If I were you—' But Horatio Smythe was no longer listening.

He pushed on down the steps. They were littered with abandoned weapons. A *pompon rouge* sprawled over the stairs, maudlin drunk, singing that haunting song of that year, '*J'attendrai*'. The bigger of the two commandos gave the singer a hearty kick in his ribs, crying, 'Come on, you drunken sod, move it, gildy!' The drunk turned under the impact and blew the burly soldier a wet kiss. The commando shook his head in mock wonder and said, 'What can yer expect, sir, from a race that makes love with their lips.'

But Smythe wasn't listening. He had spotted what he was looking for: the door to some sort of an office, bearing the gold-painted legend on it, *Etat-Major*. Headquarters. If that bastard Mercier was to be found anywhere, it would be here. He gripped his revolver more firmly and commanded, 'Follow me, chaps,' dimly aware as he did so of the muted cheering outside. For what, he didn't know,

He thrust open the door, revolver ready to fire. He stopped dead. Mercier was there all right. There was no mistaking his lean figure, clad in the immaculate white summer uniform of a French naval officer. But there was something different about

173

the admiral, as he stood gazing out of a parapet window, smoking silently. He turned and Smythe saw what it was.

Admiral Mercier had adapted to the new state of affairs in French North Africa rapidly. The Vichy insignia had gone. Wrapped round his upper right arm was a brassard bearing the legend 'FFI', and on his chest above the three rows of medal ribbons, he now wore a heart-shaped enamel badge. It featured an unusual cross that Smythe had seen before, in London, but which he couldn't immediately identify.

Then he had it. It was the Cross of Lorraine, as worn by the followers of the head of the French in exile, General de Gaulle. His grip on the revolver wavered. What the hell was going on, he asked himself.

Mercier enlightened him. His cruel face lit up into a mockery of a welcoming smile. '*Ah, mon cher monsieur Smythe.*' He fumbled for a mere moment with the Englishman's name. He stretched out his arms in a Gallic gesture of welcome. '*Maintenant, nous sommes camarades—*'

'You're no fucking comrade of mine!' Smythe retorted hotly, jerking up the muzzle of the revolver to stop Mercier moving closer.

Behind him, the two commandos looked shocked at the young officer's use of such obscenities. Smythe was beyond caring. He raised the revolver again. He pointed it straight at Mercier's evil heart, his forefinger whitening, as he took first pressure. 'Say your prayers, you bastard!' he said in English, not even bothering to try to put his words into French. 'Because you've got only a minute before I blow you to hell.'

If Mercier didn't understand the English, he certainly did the deadly look in the young Englishman's eyes. Yet he didn't seem afraid. He even managed a brief smile. '*Nous sommes des amis – we are friends,*' he said simply, as if that explained everything. '*Pour la liberté, et contre le sale cochon, Adolf Hitler!*'

The words took Smythe's breath away. Yet they didn't deflect from his purpose here, with the crowds cheering and an American band blaring away with that old World War One song, accompanied by some drunken GIs singing the words, '*Over there . . . Have a care, for the Yanks are coming . . . Over there . . .*'

174

Smythe was not listening. Now he was consumed by even stronger burning rage. He felt himself gasping with the fury of it all. The bastard thought he could change sides just like that, wash his hands of his filthy murderous past just because he had not rocked the boat and had accepted the new masters. God Almighty, what kind of world was it where people could do things like that and think they could get away with it? Was this what they were fighting for? Had Gloria – or even poor Al – died before they had begun to live to let bastards like Mercier escape their just punishment and probably die nice and comfortably of old age in bed?

'Die!' he cried, not even feeling melodramatic by the use of the word. His finger took the last trigger pressure. For the first time Mercier's face showed fear. His well-manicured hands flew to his face as if to ward off the bullet. *Crash!* The explosion reverberated round and round the little office. But the hard hand which had struck Smythe's in the very moment he had pulled the trigger had deflected his shot. His bullet slammed into the wall just to the right of Mercier's head. Plaster erupted on to the floor in the same instant that Mercier lost control of his bladder out of fear and the front of his immaculate white uniform trousers turned dark with urine.

For a moment there was a heavy echoing silence in the office, the four men frozen into position like cheap actors at the final curtain of some third-rate melodrama. Then, suddenly, startlingly, all was noise and chaos, with the major, who had knocked Smythe's hand and spoiled his aim, crying, 'Sorry, old bean. It could have been a ruddy court-martial for you if you'd shot the bugger,' and someone yelling in French, 'A towel for the admiral . . . *vite* . . . *vite* . . .' And Mercier standing there, with the urine still trickling down the inside of his trouser leg, looking pale yet confident, a little smile on his cruel face, knowing that he had won after all. He had served France, then Germany; now, it appeared, he would start serving America. It wouldn't be too difficult, he reasoned. The Americans were, he had heard, an innocent, gullible people.

He licked his lips and started his new career as an ally. The words in English came slowly and hesitantly – after all, he

175

had not spoken English since he had left his *lycée* so long ago – but he was trying at least. As the drunken sergeant patted the towel against his wet pants carefully, though he did not seem to notice at this historic moment, he said: 'Welcome, gentlemen, to French North Africa . . .'

Envoi
Duncan Harding

'But why didn't you kill Mercier there and then, Admiral?' I asked. 'Nobody but the commando CO would have known. And I doubt very much if he'd have broken down and cried at the loss. After all, Mercier's people *had* killed some of his commandos.'

Vice-Admiral Horatio Smythe took a sip of his pink gin. Even in his old age – and he was over eighty now – he liked his old naval tipple. 'It's an intriguing thought, Harding,' he answered thoughtfully, and when he spoke you could hear the wet rattle of his lungs, which indicated he was really very old. 'It'd look quite good in my obit in *The Times*. No, these days, probably the *Telegraph*. *The Times* has gone pretty bolshy, hasn't it?' He looked at me quizzically with his faded blue eyes.

I didn't know whether he was having me on or not. With the kind of advances my publisher pays, I can hardly afford the bloody *Sun*, never mind *The Times*, bolshy or otherwise.

'Yes,' the Admiral continued, the gin flushing his wrinkled old face as he sat there, stick between his legs, in the old shabby panelled room of 'Spyglass House', from which it was his habit to watch the ships passing up and down the Channel. 'That might pep up my obituary a little, eh? "Dead Admiral shot French Admiral back in '42." Someone might take it upon himself to write my biography.' He shook his head a little sadly. 'Though I doubt it. The nation's forgotten us, except when they want to trot us out, all blazers and medals, for some anniversary or other, but there won't be too many more D-Days and the like, I fear. My generation's about finished.' He gave another of those dreadful wet coughs

177

of his, which indicated that, in his case, that wasn't too far off.

'But why didn't you?' I persisted, knowing as I did so that the admiral and his kind didn't like to be harassed in this manner. It stamped me anyway as being a pleb. Posh people of the admiral's class didn't do things like that. But, though I liked the old boy a lot, it didn't matter. I wanted to get to the truth, if there was any.

'I mean, he had Jem killed and he was instrumental in killing that young American officer.' I clicked my fingers with irritation as I tried to remember the name of the commandos' US liaison officer.

'Al, you mean,' the admiral said, and suddenly rose, his bones creaking, with the aid of his stick, and I knew immediately I had pushed too hard. I've interviewed a lot of these old boys and I've found out that some don't bloody well know what they had for breakfast, but will rabbit on for hours about what happened in Kohima in '44. Then there's the other type, who are easily deflected. Perhaps it's a defensive mechanism, a way of avoiding answering questions they don't like. Now, as the admiral started to creak his way, bent heavily over the metal NHS stick, to the Regency window table, I knew I'd put my foot in it. The old admiral was going to dodge the column.

For a moment he supported himself at the table with his free hand, breathing hard. Outside, in the Channel, there was the mournful wail of a ship's siren, as the grey wet fog began to roll in. It was going to be one of those grim November days, when the world outside seemed to die and people thought of what lay before them and told themselves they might as well snuff it here and now.

A little unsteadily he took up the silver-framed photograph he sought and hobbled back to me, dropping heavily into his chair with the seat underneath that contained a pisspot – just in case he was caught short, as a lot of old boys are. Panting hard, he held it up for me with a hand covered in liver spots. 'Al and I back in Gib that November before the commando sailed for Algiers.'

I wasn't really interested, but I didn't want to offend the

old boy. After all, he had offered me lunch – one of those things in metal containers that the good ladies of the WVS supply to old boys like the admiral, awful crap – fish and taties would have been tons better. Mind you, he had been generous enough with the old pink gin.

Horatio Smythe, plain old Lieutenant Horatio Smythe as he had been then. I recognized him. He was attempting to smile as he looked into the sun, but he wasn't managing it too well. The face remained stern and worried and the American uniform he had been ordered to wear for the landing didn't fit his skinny frame.

Al, the dead American, looked totally different. His left arm was slung around Smythe's shoulders, as if they were the best of friends, who had known each other for years instead of days. The other clasped his pisspot helmet to his side like some crusader of the Middle Ages might have done just before he sallied forth in the name of God to slay the infidel under the blazing sun of darkest Africa.

But it was the long-dead American's face which really caught my attention. It was handsome, with, of course, perfect, brilliant-white teeth like all Yanks have, not the dingy old stumps that my generation were left with after the NHS dentists had done their worst. However, it was the look in Al's eyes that intrigued me most. Even that poor yellowing photo of over sixty years ago now couldn't hide that look of over-whelming confidence that shone from them. They reflected no hesitation, no doubt, no European fear that something might go wrong with the mission on which he and Smythe were about to embark.

Admiral Smythe laughed, cackled would be a better word. It was a strange sound coming from such an old man as he was. But I hadn't time to remark upon it, for he said, surprisingly, 'You see it too, don't you, Harding?'

'What sir?' I stuttered, even forgetting the old hack's principle of never saying 'sir' to anyone; I wasn't in the business of making anyone feel important.

'The look on poor Al's face. Typical American, you know. They knew they were new boys then – no experience – but they knew they were winners, too. We might have laughed at

179

them, behind their backs of course, because they were already becoming our bosses. We thought them naïve, inexperienced in war at times, hardly knowing where they were fighting and for what. But all the same they were animated by the knowledge they were Americans, and that the Yanks, as we called them then, always won. Many a time they didn't, of course. But in the end they always did one way or another. I—' He couldn't continue any further. He was suddenly attacked by that frightening, wheezing cough of his which racked the whole of his frail body, his cheeks flushing an alarming pink. I forgot my questions. Hurriedly I reached for the water jug which he always kept on the window table. But, as shaken as he was, feverishly attempting to get his breath, it was clear he didn't want to drink the tepid water. Instead he pointed a shaking skinny finger at the half-empty bottle of gin.

I understood and swiftly poured him a good measure. Whatever else the old boy was, I told myself in admiration as I did so, he was certainly going to stick to the old Royal Navy ways. A real man didn't drink water; it turned 'yer innards rusty'. A real man drank gin.

I waited as he took a couple of hearty sips of the alcohol and the hectic colour slowly departed from his raddled cheeks. Outside, the fog was growing thicker and I knew I'd have to get back to Dover soon before they started cancelling the trains to London. Finally he managed to croak, 'I'm afraid it was a bit of a wasted journey for you, Harding . . . Couldn't help you much with your latest bit of scribbling . . .'

On any other occasions I would have taken exception to that 'scribbling'. We hacks have our pride, too, you know. Well, sometimes. But not with the old admiral. My guess was that he'd be dead by the end of the year, and with his passing would vanish all he knew and had experienced, a bloody sight more than me. So I left it there. I got my story and that was that. Why bother a dying man any further?

I drained my pink gin, got my coat and said my goodbyes. He seemed hardly to hear. He didn't see me to the door. He couldn't, and I was glad he couldn't. I didn't want to linger in that old run-down place on the cliff any longer. Suddenly it smelled of death.

Outside, the fog was clammy and cold. Gulls, driven inland by it, were diving here and there, looking for scraps on the cliff top, screeching and wailing like children seeking a lost mother. I shivered and wished I could be in North Africa this November like the admiral had been in that November of 1942. I'd even chance my neck to get a bit of sunshine and warmth. But on the rest of the advance I'd get for my latest 'epic', as my publisher calls my books whenever he's attempting to talk me into another for the peanuts he forks out, I'd be lucky if I could afford a trip back to the old woman in North Shields.

As I tramped down the track, head tucked into the collar of my coat against the cold, hoping that I still had enough money left to buy one of those bloody expensive mini-bottles of whisky they sell on the trains, I remembered the comment made by a major with the British 78th Division who had gone in with the Yanks that November. God knows why, really, but then, as you may have noted, gentle reader, I haven't gone particularly overboard about the Yanks' performance in their first campaign in the Middle East. Anyway, the long-dead major of the 'Battle-Axe' Division, Taylor, his name was, I think, wrote afterwards: 'They were incorrigibly optimistic. They were unlike anyone else in the speed with which they put things right, if and when they were ordered, persuaded, or led to do so. They simply weren't prepared to lose.'

Well, I told myself as the dampness started to penetrate my shabby old coat, since then they've lost several times over. But let's hope that long-dead British major was right, and in the end they *will* put things right.

Down below in Dover, there was the deep hoot of another cross-Channel ferry entering the old harbour. That meant the train for London, crammed with passengers, legal or otherwise, would be leaving soon. I quickened my pace, the old admiral, the 'Battle-Axe' major and North Africa forgotten in my haste.

I was meeting my publisher for dinner in one of those posh places where the waiters give each other tips (a joke, gentle reader). He'd offer me a 'new epic', I was sure of that. Muggins me, I'd accept, whatever it was. I'd have to. I passed a couple of dark-skinned blokes hiding in a ditch. They looked at me;

I looked at them. What did it matter? Let immigration and the poor buggers who, in due course, would have to finance them, worry about 'em. My problem was what kind of advance my publisher would offer when we reached the cognac stage and he thought I was pissed enough. Oh well, as they said in that Latin tag I learned in my grammar school before I got the 'order of the boot' – *money don't stink . . .*

BLAYNEY

C		
C		
R		
R		
C	9/05	
N		